CW00959355

Christmas
MURDER

An Eliza Thomson Investigates

Murder Mystery

By

VL McBeath

A Christmas Murder

By VL McBeath

For more about this author please visit:
https://vlmcbeath.com

https://vlmcbeath.com/contact/

*

Editing services provided by Susan Cunningham
(www.perfectproseservices.com)
Cover design by Michelle Abrahall
(www.michelleabrahall.com)

ISBNs:

978-1-9161340-2-7 (Kindle Edition)
978-1-9161340-3-4 (Paperback)

Main category - FICTION / Historical Mysteries
Other category - FICTION / Crime & Mystery

CHAPTER ONE

London, December 1901

Eliza Thomson sat in the back of her husband's carriage, peering out of the window. She hadn't realised how quickly the evening was drawing in until a fork of lightning illuminated the rooftops in the tree-lined streets of Richmond upon Thames. The rain started before the rumble of thunder reached them and she pulled the collar of her cloak higher around her neck.

Her friend Connie leaned forward to stare at the gloom. "Does the weather not realise it's nearly Christmas? Those clouds should be full of snow by now."

Eliza shuddered as the gentle patter of rain turned into a torrent, pummelling the cobbled street and drowning out all but the sound of the horses' hooves as they quickened their pace. "I don't think it's cold enough to snow but there's still time. Don't give up hope."

She let out a low shriek as the speed of the horses caused her to topple towards the corner of the carriage. "Good gracious, this driver needs to slow down. We'll be there in a minute even if he doesn't go at such a pace." She flinched as the momentum caused Connie to slide along the bench and collide with her.

"My goodness, what's going on?" Connie pushed herself back to her own side of the carriage.

"I don't suppose the horses want to get wet any more than we do."

Eliza's husband Archie turned in his seat to study the horses. "I don't know about them, but I'm sure the drivers would rather they weren't sitting outside in this. They have a grand job in the summer, but I wouldn't swap with them tonight."

"Me neither." Eliza jumped as a second bolt of lightning flashed crossed the sky. "At least Father will have something arranged for them once we get there. The stables will be ready to drive straight into and the hip flask will be waiting."

"Let's hope so…" A crash of thunder, much closer than the first, drowned out the rest of Archie's reply.

"We'll be sleeping with the horses at this rate," Connie said as the noise dissipated. "We won't even be able to walk across the yard without catching our death of cold."

"It's not far," Archie said. "No more than twenty paces, and I brought this." He reached under the seat and pulled out a neatly folded umbrella.

"I've a feeling we'll need more than that." Eliza's attention drifted back to the horses, who had slowed to a trot as they navigated the driveway of a large, red-brick detached house. As they approached the backyard, a coachman dressed in an oversized mackintosh and wide-brimmed hat hurried from an outhouse to direct them to the stables.

Once they were at a standstill, Archie jumped down from the carriage. "I'd say we got here in the nick of time." He squinted out into the gloom. "This storm looks like it's here for the night. I'll run inside and see if your father has any more umbrellas."

A minute later, Archie returned and ushered the ladies across the stone flags, through the back door and into the kitchen.

"What a horrible evening." Eliza shook the excess water from her cloak as a maid took the umbrella from her. "We'd better leave the luggage in the carriage until the rain eases. I don't want the presents ruined before anyone has the chance to unwrap them."

"I'm sure they'll be fine; I'm not going to let anything spoil Christmas." A smile lit up Connie's face as she passed her own coat to the maid. "It's going to be special this year. I wonder if Mr Bell's put up the decorations yet. I hope he's left something for us to do."

"He has plenty of decorations up already, madam," the maid said. "He wanted the house to be at its best when you arrived, but I'm sure we can find space for a few more. If you'd like to go up, Mr Bell's waiting for you in the drawing room. He asked me to serve afternoon tea as soon as you arrived."

"Splendid." Eliza linked her arm through Connie's. "He always knew how to spoil me. Come on, let's go and surprise him." She led the way from the kitchen, up the stairs to the front hallway where she stopped by a large mirror. "After being outside in that weather, I'd better take a look at myself." She removed her feather-trimmed hat, scowling as several strands of dark brown hair broke free from their grips. "I'd swear this hair has a mind of its own. Yours never moves."

"Oh, it does." Connie waited behind her. "You just never see it. You need more hairpins, that's the secret. Your hair's too thick to manage with the number you put in. I'm sure Dr Thomson will buy you some if you ask him nicely."

Eliza raised her eyebrows. "Less of your cheek. I'm perfectly capable of buying my own hairpins without involving Archie."

The words were no sooner out of her mouth than Archie joined them. "What aren't you going to involve me in?"

Eliza grinned. "Nothing you need worry about; now come along, Father will be waiting."

Mr Bell jumped from his seat as Eliza and Connie entered the drawing room. "Here you are. I was beginning to think you'd been delayed by the storm."

"No, thankfully it only started as we turned into the road." Eliza crossed the room towards the selection of chairs that surrounded the fire and embraced her father.

"It looks like it's going to be a terrible evening," Connie said as Eliza positioned herself in front of the fire to warm her hands.

"Well, you'll be safe and dry here, my dear." Mr Bell took Connie's hand and planted a kiss on the back of it. "Ah, Archie, come on in. The tea will be here shortly."

"Thank you so much for inviting me," Connie said. "I always love Christmas, but it's not quite the same when you're on your own."

"Of course I invited you. I could hardly entertain the rest of the family and leave you alone. Now, take a seat and make yourself at home." He glanced towards the door, his brow creasing, before he turned to Eliza. "Have you not brought

Henry with you? I want to hear all about Cambridge and find out what they're teaching him."

Eliza rolled her eyes. "A final round of parties before Christmas. I really don't know how he does it, but he'll be here on Tuesday. There'll be plenty of time to talk to him then."

"Oh to be twenty again." Mr Bell sighed as he retook his seat. "Not that I had the opportunities he has, but he won't be young forever. Let him enjoy himself. You'll just have to tell me what you've been up to instead."

"I'm sure my life is terribly dull in comparison, so I shan't even try to compete, but I must say you've surpassed yourself with the decorations this year. The room looks wonderful not to mention the tree. You've been busy."

Mr Bell threw back his head as he laughed. "I didn't lift a finger as you well know. The maids like doing it. It makes a change from their usual chores."

"They haven't lit the candles on the tree yet though. Did you save that for us?" Eliza's eyes sparkled as she glanced down at her father.

He returned her smile and handed her a small box. "I know how you enjoy that bit."

Connie clapped her hands in front of her chest as she joined Eliza by the tree in the bay window. "I was hoping you'd left something for us. It would be such a dull time of year if it wasn't for Christmas, don't you think?"

"It most certainly would." Eliza held a match to the first of the six candles tied to the tree. "I just hope it doesn't get too cold."

"Surely you want it to snow?" Connie's eyes widened.

"That's different." Eliza's eyes didn't move from the tree as she searched out the next candle.

"Well, whether it does or not, you've no need to worry," Mr Bell said. "I've enough coal in the cellar to last at least two weeks."

"It's to be hoped the weather doesn't keep us here that long." Archie stretched out his legs in front of him. "I've only arranged cover for the surgery for a week."

"I'm amazed you could manage that long."

An involuntary smile crept onto Eliza's lips at the friendly tone of her father's voice.

Archie grunted. "After the misunderstanding earlier this year when I covered for Dr Wark while you all went to Lowton Hall, he was only too happy to keep an eye on things."

"So, some good came out of it then." Mr Bell paused as a maid knocked on the door and brought in a large tea tray. "Thank you, my dear. Just leave it over there and we'll deal with it."

Eliza glanced back over her shoulder as the maid placed the tray on a console table behind one of the settees and disappeared as quickly as she arrived.

"Would you like to do the honours?" Mr Bell asked her. "I'm not so good at that sort of thing."

Eliza handed Connie the matches to light the final two candles and walked back to the table. After stirring the tea in the pot, she offered around the selection of sandwiches and cakes. "Do you have anything planned for us while we're here? I had hoped to go for a walk in the park tomorrow, but unless this weather lets up, it looks like we'll be stuck indoors."

"I can help you there." Mr Bell's face lit up. "We've been invited out for luncheon."

"Luncheon? Where?"

"Only next door. You've heard me talk of Mrs Cranford? Well, she popped in earlier this week with an invitation. She claimed it was a pre-Christmas, midwinter celebration, but then let slip that someone had told her you were visiting. Apparently, she wants to meet you. I think that's the real reason we've been invited."

"Me!" Eliza put a hand to her chest as she sat down. "Why on earth would she be interested in me?"

Archie laughed. "Your fame must be preceding you, my dear."

"Don't laugh about it." Mr Bell smirked at his son-in-law. "You're nearer the truth than you realise."

"What do you mean?" Eliza studied her father as he bit into an egg sandwich.

"Oh, it's nothing to worry about. I may have mentioned to a couple of friends that you'd helped the police with some murder investigations..."

"May have mentioned?" Eliza raised an eyebrow as she handed Mr Bell a cup of tea.

"I didn't give them any details; it was just that when the newspapers reported the trials, I had to say something. You know how word travels and Mrs Cranford always likes to make sure she knows everything."

"Another Mrs Petty?" Connie asked.

"No, not at all. She's a lovely woman..."

"As is Mrs Petty," Eliza said.

"Well, quite." Mr Bell took a hasty sip of his tea. "What I mean is, Mrs Cranford's about your age and she's a marvellous hostess. There are not many people in the neighbourhood she hasn't entertained, which means she knows everyone. That's where she gets all her information from. Anyway, it turns out she has an interest in solving murders and wants to meet you."

"Well, what can I say? I'm sure I don't want to bore the rest of the guests with tales of murder, especially not at this time of year when we're all supposed to be jolly."

Mr Bell chuckled. "You've no need to worry about that. Mrs Cranford is always the life and soul of the party; she won't let it turn morbid. Knowing her, she'll have a list of questions as long as your arm about each of the murders and how you solved them."

"Does she not have a husband to stop all this nonsense?" Archie helped himself to another small triangular sandwich.

"She does. Nice chap too, but he's about as effective constraining her as you are with Eliza."

"Father!" Eliza shot Mr Bell a ferocious look. "We're not just here to be your housekeepers, you should have realised that by now."

"My dear, when have I ever stopped you doing exactly what you want? I was merely suggesting that Mrs Cranford has the same spirit as you."

"What does Mr Cranford do for a living?" Archie asked.

"He owns the new department store on Oxford Street, Cranford's."

"Really?" Connie's eyes lit up. "I've heard about that. It's supposed to be rather grand. Do you think we could make a visit while we're here?"

"I'm sure we could arrange that," Mr Bell said.

"I don't know when." Eliza's brow furrowed. "We obviously can't go tomorrow, and I had planned to go to the theatre on Tuesday afternoon. There's a new musical production that's just started at the Vaudeville. I was going to treat Connie as a Christmas present."

"My, that sounds wonderful too." Connie's smile lit up her face. "Do you think we'd be able to squeeze in a trip to Cranford's as well? I don't suppose we'll want to travel into London on Monday as well as Tuesday."

"It depends on the weather," Archie said. "If the rain doesn't stop, you might not even want to travel in once."

"Of course we will." Eliza grinned at her friend. "Whether it rains or not, we'll either be in the theatre or in the shop. We needn't come out for hours. Isn't that right, Connie?"

"Oh, at least three hours in each I would say."

Archie groaned. "Well, it's a good job I brought a couple of books with me. I'm happy to go to the theatre but I hope you don't mind if I excuse myself from a whole morning of shopping."

"As long as you give the cashier instructions to set up an account for me, I won't mind at all."

Mr Bell grimaced at his son-in-law. "I'd say you'd be better going with them. At least then you'll be able to keep an eye on them."

"Don't encourage him," Eliza said. "We'll be perfectly happy on our own."

Archie reached for a buttered scone. "That's the worry."

CHAPTER TWO

B y the time Eliza and Connie arrived in the dining room the following morning, Mr Bell was waiting for them. The rain of the previous evening had subsided to a steady drizzle, but the wind rattled around the windows causing the curtains to quiver with each gust.

"Where's Archie? He must have come downstairs a good hour ago." Eliza moved into the chair Mr Bell held out for her.

"He got fed up waiting for you and so popped outside to check on the horses. He'll be back in a minute."

"What a cheek! He should try putting on a corset and six layers of petticoats when he gets dressed."

Mr Bell chuckled. "I'm sure that would make an interesting sight. Why don't you help yourselves to some of those sausages before he comes back?"

Eliza smiled. "We shouldn't start without him, although I suppose they will go cold. You two may, I'm not terribly hungry, and if we're out for luncheon, I don't want too much to eat in advance. What are the arrangements for the day?"

Mr Bell's shoulders sagged. "It's Sunday. We go to church, remember."

Eliza let out a deep breath. "Yes, I'm aware of that; I mean afterwards."

"Mrs Cranford wants us at one o'clock."

"One o'clock!" Archie closed the door behind him as he joined them. "That won't give us long to get back here, especially if you two dally as much in church as you do when you're getting dressed."

Eliza glared at her husband. "You know, one of these days I will make him put on six petticoats and see how he manages."

"Well, not today," Mr Bell said. "We can go in the carriage and that will give us an extra few minutes."

"Won't Mrs Cranford be in church?" Eliza asked.

Mr Bell studied his pocket watch. "She'll probably be there already, knowing her. She organises the hymn books and the collection plates before everyone arrives. She keeps the place running."

"I'm surprised she has the time if she's hosting a luncheon as well."

"She has a wonderful cook and a couple of good maids. She leaves everything to them."

"Lucky her." Eliza stood up and poured them all a cup of tea.

"What can you tell us about the other guests?" Connie asked.

"Not a lot, if I'm being honest. I've no idea who's been invited although I imagine the Cranford's neighbours on the other side, Mr and Mrs McRae, will be there. Mrs McRae is never out of the Cranfords' house, not while Mr Cranford's at work at any rate. The thing is, she's a strange woman; I can't fathom her out at all."

Archie almost choked on his tea. "I'm sure that's not the first time a man's said that about a woman."

Mr Bell failed to see the funny side. "Maybe not, but you mark my words, she's very peculiar. I expect Mrs Cranford will alternate the ladies and men around the dining table and so I wouldn't laugh until you find out who you're sitting next to."

It was turned half past twelve by the time Mr Bell's carriage returned from church and pulled into the backyard. As it did, Eliza peered out at the grey sky.

"I think this is as light as it's going to get today. It's a good job we don't have far to walk after luncheon. At this rate, it'll be dark when we leave, and the moon won't make any impression through these clouds."

"Didn't you notice our new streetlights? They're a lot brighter than the old gas lamps."

"I did, as it happens, but I haven't seen them lit." Eliza sighed. "I don't suppose we'll be getting them in Moreton for a while."

"We don't need them," Connie said. "The gas lamps are perfectly good enough. Who wants bright lights blazing all night?"

"Not you, obviously. Come on, let's get into the house. Hopefully Cook will have a pot of tea waiting for us. We've made good time, and we needn't go next door for another half an hour or so."

Mr Bell shook his head. "There's no 'or so' about it. Mrs Cranford may be friendly, but she is a stickler for punctuality. We need to be there at one o'clock on the dot."

Connie laughed. "The way she was still talking to everyone when we left church, I doubt she'll be home herself by then."

"Oh, she will. Didn't you see Mr Cranford waiting outside in their carriage? They'll have arrived back while we've been sitting here."

Half an hour later, huddled beneath several umbrellas, Mr Bell led them up the Cranfords' driveway. The house was of similar design to his, with a large bay window to the right of the front door and the attic rooms nestling snugly within the tiles of the roof. They arrived just in time to see the door open and their fellow guests step inside.

"Anyone you know?" Eliza whispered.

"I do and fortunately I get on with them well enough. I'll be surprised if that's all she's invited though." He glanced over his shoulder. "The others must either have been early or they're late."

A maid waited for them to reach the hallway before closing the door and taking their wet things.

"Mr Bell, I thought I recognised your voice." An immaculately dressed woman wearing a frilled blouse over a fluted skirt walked towards them, her shoes clipping on the terracotta floor tiles.

"Mrs Cranford, how lovely you look." Mr Bell took the hand she offered him and kissed the back. "Let me introduce the family."

Mrs Cranford wore a broad smile as Eliza stepped forward. "Mrs Thomson, how delightful to meet you at last. I'm so sorry I didn't have a chance to talk to you in church, but you know how it is. One has to divide one's attention between everyone."

Eliza returned her smile. "Please, think nothing of it, Mrs Cranford. Given we were coming for luncheon, it was quite right you spent time with everyone else."

"Now, please, no more Mrs Cranford, it sounds so formal. All my friends call me Rosamund."

"My, I'm honoured, but only if you call me Eliza."

Rosamund put a hand on Eliza's shoulder. "I should be delighted to, and this must be Mr Bell's other guest."

Eliza took Connie by the arm and pulled her into the conversation. "This is my good friend and next-door neighbour, Mrs Connie Appleton. She's helped in a lot of murder cases I've been involved with."

"Really?" Rosamund's eyes sparkled. "How very exciting. I'm so looking forward to you telling me all about them, although I suppose I'd better do my duty as hostess first. Let me introduce you to everyone." She linked her arm through Eliza's and led her down the hall towards the drawing room. The door was open as they approached, and Eliza peered inside to see a room in sharp contrast to the hall with its wood panelling and dark colours. On the far wall were two large windows overlooking the garden with an extraordinarily tall Christmas tree between them decorated with an array of baubles and candles. The light reflected off the pale walls giving the illusion of brightness, even on this darkest of days. The furniture consisted of an elegant selection of chairs, which were placed in small groups around the room.

"Betty, look who's here." Rosamund ushered them towards a woman of similar age and stature to herself, who was in front of the fire talking to an elderly couple.

"This is Mr Bell's daughter, Mrs Eliza Thomson. Do you remember, I was telling you about her? Eliza, this is my neighbour, Mrs Betty McRae, and her next-door neighbours, Mr and Mrs Reed."

"Pleased to meet you," Eliza said. "This is my companion, Mrs Connie Appleton."

A smile beamed across Rosamund's face as she pulled Connie into the group. "Connie's another one who does some sleuthing. Isn't it thrilling?"

"Ridiculous if you want my opinion." Mr Reed stood up straight with his hands behind his back. "Not at all the sort of thing women should be involved with."

"Oh Ros, darling, he's right. Why do you get so excited about things like this?" Betty's smile slipped into a pout. "I'm sure it's frightfully tedious."

"It has its moments." Eliza forced her smile to stay on her lips as she glanced between the two women. "But I'm sure we'll try not to bore you with any of the details if you're not interested."

Betty pursed her lips. "Oh, I'll hear all about it, anyway. Rosamund obviously failed to mention that as well as being her neighbour, we're very close friends. We go everywhere together, don't we, Ros?"

Rosamund put a hand on her friend's shoulder. "We do. Everywhere."

"You must forgive me then if you thought me rude in church this morning." A frown settled on Eliza's brow. "I'd swear I didn't see you."

The smile on Betty's face disappeared and the look in her eyes became unreadable as she stared at a tall gentleman with dark hair standing beside the Christmas tree. "There's no need to apologise, I wasn't able to make it this morning. Something cropped up."

"I'm sure we all miss a service from time to time..." Eliza stopped when the man who was the object of Betty's attention glanced across the room and made his way towards them. A second, shorter man with greying hair joined him.

As soon as they were within touching distance, Rosamund extended her arm and pulled the second gentleman into the group.

"And about time too," she said to him. "It's awfully rude to stand on the other side of the room when we have guests. Eliza, Connie, this is my husband Mr Cranford. Darling, this is the Mrs Thomson I was telling you about, and her friend Mrs Appleton."

Mr Cranford gave the ladies a slight bow before extending his hand to Mr Bell, who stood behind them. "Glad you could make it, old chap. This must be your son-in-law."

Mr Bell chuckled. "There's no fooling you, I see. Yes, this is Dr Thomson. Unfortunately, we couldn't persuade my grandson Henry to give up his party this weekend. He's up at Cambridge at the moment and sounds like he's making the most of it."

"Well, it's very nice to meet you, Dr Thomson." Mr Cranford offered him his hand. "Please excuse my wife, but she's been so excited about meeting Mrs Thomson that I believe she's forgotten to introduce everyone else."

"No need to apologise, I'm sure. I know how excitable women can be." Archie smirked at Eliza when she glared at him.

"Well, it's still no excuse. Now, let me finish the introductions." He brought the taller man into the discussion. "This is Mr Cameron McRae, my next-door neighbour and husband to the lovely Betty here. Not that he sees much of her given she's always here."

The two couples laughed, but the pause in the conversation was a second too long. Archie hurriedly extended his hand to Mr McRae. "Pleased to meet you."

"Aye, and you too."

Mr Cranford patted his neighbour on the back. "I say. It sounds as if you and Dr Thomson have something in common, Cameron. Are you Scottish, Dr Thomson?"

"I am indeed," Archie said, "although I didn't think anyone would still be able to tell after all my years in and around London. I imagine with a name like McRae it's not so easy to hide. Have you been down here long?"

"Longer than I care to remember!" Mr McRae's jawline relaxed, and he allowed a smile to cross his lips. "I came down here for a job, met Betty and never went back."

"That sounds familiar." Archie laughed. "I don't know how these women do it."

"Oh yes you do." Rosamund beamed at them. "They are simply so irresistible that you couldn't bear to be parted from them. Now, before we say anything else, let me thank you all for coming to our little winter solstice luncheon. Not that we celebrate it, of course, but as it's today, I thought we should have a drink to mark the occasion."

As if on cue a maid arrived carrying a silver tray containing a selection of glasses and a large jug.

"Oh my, that smells good." Connie sniffed at the aroma. "Mulled wine I would say, with cinnamon and cloves. It always reminds me of Christmas."

Rosamund smiled as she walked to the table where the maid was setting down the tray. "You're absolutely right, and what better time to drink it. The weather's been so dreadful that I decided a warm drink would be much more appropriate than a gin punch ... and we didn't want tea!" She laughed at her own joke.

"You always do the right thing." Betty moved to Rosamund's side as the maid filled each glass and handed them to her mistress.

"Eliza, let me give you the first glass but be careful with it, it's still hot. Not that it will take long to cool. Connie, you have this next one."

"What wonderful glass holders." Eliza held the delicate handle as she fingered the intricate detail on the sterling silver bases.

"Aren't they just? Mr Cranford recently ordered some for the store and allowed me to have a set as a present. Unfortunately, I only have six and so the men will have to mind their fingers." She tittered to herself as she handed around the rest of the glasses.

"What is it you do down here?" Archie asked Mr McRae once they'd both received their drinks.

"I'm an engineer. I design bridges for the railways."

Eliza blew across the top of her drink. *Not more railways.*

Archie nodded. "I suppose they're laying a lot more track down here than they are back home."

"They're not doing badly in Scotland, especially as the weather's often bad up there, but they can't get enough men down here and so the pay's better. Not that I'm complaining."

"Excuse me for interrupting." Eliza placed a hand on Mr McRae's arm. "I think Rosamund wants to say something."

With her glass raised in the air, Rosamund tapped the side with a small silver spoon. "Can I propose a toast for our little gathering and wish you all a peaceful midwinter's day? Let us also give thanks that from tomorrow the days will start getting longer again."

"Hear hear." Betty bounced on the spot as she raised her glass. "Thank you to our wonderful Rosamund for having us here today."

Mr McRae followed suit. "To a peaceful midwinter's day."

"Why didn't you join my toast to Rosamund?" Betty glared at her husband as everyone followed his lead.

Mr McRae's eyes narrowed as he stared back at Betty. "It was hardly a toast, it was just a thank you."

"It was still worth repeating..."

Mr Bell stepped forward and raised his glass. "To our wonderful hostess, Mrs Cranford. Thank you for having us."

Rosamund flashed a broad smile as she acknowledged the toast and after taking a mouthful of wine she moved towards Mr Bell, who stood between Eliza and Connie.

"Mr Bell, that was very sweet of you. You have a lovely father, Eliza."

"Yes, I'm very fortunate." Eliza's smile disappeared as Betty pushed past her, almost causing her to spill her drink.

"Oh, my dear, I'm so sorry." Rosamund picked up a napkin to wipe Eliza's dress. "Did it go on your skirt?"

"No, I don't think so ... although wearing such a dark red means that even if it did, it won't stain. Let's not worry about it."

"Well, I must apologise for my friend. I'm sure I've no idea what's got into her." Rosamund turned to Mr Bell. "Would you mind awfully if I stole Eliza from you for a few minutes? I've been dying to talk to her all week and I have a suggestion I want to put to her."

"Not at all. Mr Reed and I are only talking about the changes to the South Eastern Railway since the merger."

Mr Reed shook his head. "Terrible business it was too..."

Eliza rolled her eyes. "Oh, please, Rosamund, lead me somewhere else. I'd really rather not listen to that."

Rosamund giggled as she led Eliza and Connie away from the fire. "These men and their trains, they never seem to tire of them."

"Don't I know it."

"Now, before we take a seat, let me top your glasses up and then you can tell me about your sleuthing. I want to hear all about it."

CHAPTER THREE

Rosamund led them to the drinks table before they continued to a collection of seats near the Christmas tree.

"Now then, what can you tell me?" Rosamund adjusted her skirt to make herself comfortable. "How do you always manage to work out who the murderer is?"

"There's not much to tell, really. It's just a matter of keeping your eyes and ears open."

"I'm sure it's not." Connie's cheeks were red. "If ever there's a murder to investigate, I spend most of my time with Eliza, but I don't see or hear half the things she does."

"That's because you're not paying attention, dear." Eliza patted her friend's hand.

"I pay as much attention as you, more sometimes. If you remember, I often recap what we've learned, but I never put all the pieces together and come up with the right answer."

"What are you doing, starting without me?" Betty was at Rosamund's side, her eyes boring into her. "I thought you said you were going to talk to them in the morning room. I was waiting for you in there."

Rosamund stood up and offered Betty her chair. "I'm sorry, dear, but after the exit you made, I didn't think you'd be joining us. But never mind, I apologised to Eliza for you and she was about to let us into some of her secrets."

"You don't need to know any of that, Ros. You'll be perfectly capable of working things out yourself if you ever need to solve a murder, which I'm sure you never will."

A gleam flitted across Rosamund's eyes. "That's where you're wrong, my dear; now, don't be such a killjoy and sit down, you might learn something yourself."

Eliza sat up straight. "What are you thinking?"

Rosamund laughed. "Oh, don't worry, dear, I'm not about to murder anyone. I'm just teasing Betty here, because she can be frightfully miserable if she thinks I'm having fun and she's not. Now, tell us, how do you catch these murderers?"

"Well, as I was saying, it's about being alert, listening to what people have to say ... and just as importantly being aware of what they don't say. As long as you pay attention, it's really not that difficult." Eliza stopped when Connie tutted beside her. "What's that for?"

Connie rolled her eyes at Rosamund. "It may be easy for her because she happens to be rather clever. Did Mr Bell tell you that she went to university when she was younger and has a degree in science?"

Rosamund's eyes were wide. "Really? No. Why didn't he tell me? He's always talking about you, but he never mentioned that. Is that how you manage to pick up on things other people miss?"

Eliza shrugged. "I'm sure I don't know, although it could

be because I have an analytical mind. Anyone can learn how to do it. Connie's doing well enough, aren't you?"

"It's not terribly ladylike, being analytical." Betty rolled her shoulders. "Men prefer ladies who don't ask too many questions."

"Of course they do!" Eliza laughed. "That way they keep themselves to themselves while they find out everything about us. Wouldn't you rather have a husband who didn't ask questions?"

Rosamund joined in Eliza's laughter. "Oh, Eliza, you are funny. Mr Bell tells me you *work* as well."

"I do. Once my son went up to Cambridge, I needed something to occupy my time. Shortly after he left, we moved to Moreton and Archie had a vacancy for an apothecary for the surgery. Since I have my science degree it seemed like a solution to both our problems. Plus, he doesn't have to pay me as much money as if he hired someone in."

Connie nudged her. "You get more than enough with new dresses. I'm sure Dr Thomson wouldn't be buying them for any other helper."

"I should hope not!" Eliza drained the mulled wine from the bottom of her glass and placed a hand on her chest. "Oh my, that wine's gone straight to my head. I'd better not have any more."

"Nonsense, a little top-up won't do you any harm." Rosamund stood up and took Eliza and Connie's glasses from them. "Now, don't go telling Betty any secrets while I'm away. I'll be back in two ticks."

Betty's face was like thunder as Rosamund left.

"Have you known Rosamund long?" Eliza asked when Rosamund showed no immediate signs of returning.

"Long enough." The same unreadable expression had settled in Betty's eyes as she watched Rosamund pour three glasses of wine.

"She probably couldn't carry four glasses." Eliza forced a smile as she nodded towards Betty's glass.

"Yes, you're right. I'll go and help her."

Before Eliza could respond, Betty had gone.

"Good grief. What's that all about?" Connie asked once Betty was out of earshot.

Eliza shrugged. "I get the distinct impression that she's not happy we're here. I suspect she'd rather have Rosamund to herself, which could explain why she doesn't want her asking about the sleuthing."

Connie straightened her back. "How silly."

Eliza gave her a sideways glance. "Because you'd never do anything like that?"

"That was different." Connie wore a look of indignation that Eliza always found amusing. "All right, so maybe I wasn't being myself when Mrs Hartley was in Moreton, but I wasn't behaving as badly as Betty."

A frown settled on Connie's forehead and Eliza followed her gaze as Rosamund hurried from the drinks table to disturb the conversation between Archie and Mr McRae. With little preamble, she ushered Mr McRae into the hall leaving Betty alone peering at the door as if willing herself to see through it. Moments later the two of them returned, only for Mr McRae to escort Betty from the room.

"I'm sorry about that." Rosamund handed Eliza and Connie a glass as she rejoined them. "Betty wasn't feeling well and so I asked Cameron to help her to the front door for some fresh air. She really can't take her wine."

"What a shame," Connie said. "I thought she'd gone rather quiet. Will they join us for luncheon?"

"Oh, I imagine so." The smile disappeared from Rosamund's face. "In fact, it's about time we took our seats in the dining room. Bring your drinks with you."

By the time they'd walked back down the hall to the room with the bay window, Betty and Mr McRae were hovering around the long rectangular table.

"Ros, what were you thinking when you did the place settings? You've sat me in the middle of the table."

"I'm sorry, dear, but we have to give the seats of honour to our guests. You know that."

"That should mean Dr Thomson and Mr Bell sit next to you, but you have Mrs Thomson instead. It's all wrong."

"Eliza, will you excuse me a moment?" Rosamund moved around the table and took Betty by the arm, ushering her into the hall. A moment later, she was back. "There, that's all sorted out. We always have to rearrange the seating plan when we have an uneven number of men and women and Betty just doesn't like change. Now, will you all take your seats?"

Eliza sat to Rosamund's right-hand side with Betty's husband, Mr McRae, to her left and Archie and Connie opposite.

"This is all looking very nice, Rosamund." She indicated towards the centre of the table and the decorations of winter leaves and berries.

"Betty and I did the arrangements, didn't we, dear?" She smiled at Betty, who had silently followed her back into the room and taken her place next to Archie. "It took us most of yesterday afternoon. You should have seen my hands after tying those pieces of pine together."

"Well, I'm sure it was worth it and I imagine you'll be able to use them at Christmas too if you put them outside to keep."

"That's exactly what I'm hoping, although it will need to snow for it to be cold enough. I have my son and daughter visiting for the day. My son works in the city and my daughter married a banker, and so I only get to see them on special occasions. I must admit I'm rather looking forward to it."

"And they enjoy coming here, too," Mr McRae said. "She spoils them with kindness."

"I'm sure I don't. I'm only doing what every mother does. I imagine you treat your son, too, don't you, Eliza?"

Eliza rolled her eyes. "He doesn't know he's born with the allowance Archie gives him while he's at university. Hopefully, it will be worth it and one day he'll start spoiling me." She leaned back from the table as a plate of meat, beef it looked like under the thick gravy, was placed in front of her.

"The potatoes and vegetables won't be long," Rosamund said. "We'll have to serve ourselves, I'm afraid. I've given one of the maids the afternoon off to spend time with her family before Christmas. I hope you don't mind?"

"No, of course not. That's very generous of you. I'm sure the maid was thrilled."

"Well, these poor mites don't get home very often and so I said one could go today and the other will disappear on Boxing Day. I thought it was only fair."

"My cook and maid were delighted that we're spending Christmas here this year. They've been able to go home for a whole week. I've just asked them to get back to the house a day earlier than us so they can sort out the food, put the fires on and clear the dust away."

"What a treat for them; I honestly don't think I could do that. Everyone always comes here for Christmas and we wouldn't have it any other way."

They ate most of the meal in silence but as Eliza placed her knife and fork on her empty plate, Rosamund put a hand on her arm.

"I think it's time I let you into my little secret." Rosamund was clearly struggling to keep the excitement from her face.

"What secret?"

"The reason I was so keen to hear about your sleuthing methods. In fact, let me tell everyone together." She stood up and clapped her hands to silence the conversations. "Can I have your attention? As you're aware, we're having the family here for Christmas and so I thought it would be good fun to have some parlour games planned for Christmas evening. I was just finalising my selections when I heard that Mrs Thomson would be here for the week."

Eliza glanced at Archie. "What have I got to do with parlour games?"

"Don't you see? One of my favourite pastimes when I was a child was Murder in the Dark. Once I knew you'd be here, I wanted to learn your techniques so that I could play the detective."

Eliza breathed a sigh of relief. "Oh, I see. Well, I'm sure there's not much to it. You just need to be observant when the lights are turned back on, take note of who's standing where and then ask a few questions."

"But what sort of questions? That's what I'm struggling with and so I developed a plan. With it being the middle of winter, it will be dark by the time we've eaten dessert and so I thought we could have a game while you're here."

The heat rose in Eliza's cheeks. "You want me to play the detective?"

Rosamund laughed. "No, not at all, although the thought did occur to me before I had a better idea." Rosamund clapped her hands together under her chin. "I know that normally when you're playing Murder in the Dark everyone is dealt a hand of cards to show who'll be the detective, policeman and murder victim, but–" she paused to study her guests "–I wonder if you'd mind me being the detective."

Eliza glanced around the table to see if anyone was likely to burst Rosamund's bubble. *How can they argue with such childlike joy?*

"I'm sure we'd be delighted for you, my dear," Mr Cranford said.

"Marvellous! That way, when we play on Christmas night with the family, I'll have a head start."

"Except for Mr Cranford," Connie said.

The smile faded from Rosamund's lips as she turned to Connie. "What do you mean?"

"Well, presumably he'll be playing the game today and so he'll pick up a few tips too."

Rosamund shook her head. "No, that's absurd. You wouldn't dare, would you, dear?"

Mr Cranford smiled from the other end of the table. "Always do as I'm told, my dear. If you want me to play deaf, just let me know."

The smile returned to Rosamund's lips. "There, that was sorted out easily enough. Now, let's get this dessert eaten, and the port and mince pies served, and then we can start."

CHAPTER FOUR

There was a chill in the air when the party returned to the drawing room, but a maid had pulled the heavy velvet curtains across the windows and was loading more coal onto the fire. Within minutes, the flames were crackling and flickering in the grate as the wind howled down the chimney. The girl had clearly been told about the game ahead of the guests, because she'd extinguished the candles on the tree and pushed the occasional tables and chairs back to the walls. After a moment's confusion, the ladies wandered to the chairs closest to the fire, while the men stood together in the centre of the room.

No sooner had they settled than Rosamund breezed into the room, holding up a packet of playing cards. "Gentlemen, will you join the ladies over here so we can decide the rules we want to play by?"

Mr Cranford smiled at his wife. "I imagine you already have your own ideas, my dear. Why don't you just tell us all what you'd like us to do?"

Rosamund tittered. "Well, if you're sure you don't mind."

When there were no objections, she continued. "I presume you're all familiar with the game. The first thing we need to do is sort out who'll be the murderer and who'll be the policeman. I've taken the liberty of taking all the jokers, aces, kings and jacks from the pack." She fanned out the cards to show them around the guests. "I've added back in the ace of spades and king of hearts, and as per the usual rules, whoever has the ace will be the murderer and the policeman will be the one with the king."

"Don't you want Eliza to have the king so she can help you?" Connie asked.

Rosamund's eyes lit up. "What a wonderful idea. The policeman is usually only there to keep the suspects in order while the detective is busy, but we can change the rules so that Mrs Thomson can help me."

"Rosamund!" Betty's tone was brusque. "You're perfectly capable of working out the killer by yourself, you don't need help."

Rosamund grinned at Eliza. "Oh, but it would be so much more fun to have both of us doing it. Don't you think so, Eliza?"

Eliza shrugged. "I don't mind either way."

"Of course you do, you're just being polite. Take no notice of Betty. I've decided I'd like you to be the policeman so let me get rid of this king from the cards."

Connie's brow remained creased. "What happens if the murderer accidentally murders you, Rosamund? Normally, the person with the king would become the detective, but I suppose that defeats the purpose of the game."

"Well spotted, Connie." Rosamund beamed at her. "I had wondered about that and decided that if I am murdered, we should start again. After all, I can't keep you here all night until I get my chance to play detective."

The polite sound of laughter echoed around the room.

"No, you can't," Mr Bell said. "I need my sleep."

"And you'll get it, I'm sure. With Eliza's help, we'll identify the murderer in no time at all."

"How will we be murdered?" Mr McRae asked. "There are quite a few different ways to play."

"Hmm, yes you're right." Rosamund paused and studied her guests. "Perhaps because this is only a test, a tap on the shoulder will suffice. No whispering to the victim though. The room isn't terribly big, and the murderer is likely to be overheard."

"What about putting a hand over the victim's mouth to stop them calling out?" Mr McRae said. "That's how we usually play."

Rosamund shuddered. "No, I don't think so. It's far too aggressive and don't forget we have Mr and Mrs Reed with us. They're too old for that sort of thing. It would give them such a fright, Mrs Reed especially. And while we're on the subject of frights, no removing bodies from the room either. There are some who've started to take this game far too seriously."

Mr McRae was about to interrupt when Rosamund held up her hand. "No, a tap on the shoulder is fine and if you feel such a tap, either fall to the floor if you're able, or if not, move to the nearest chair and sit down. You need to stay where you are, quite silently, until someone finds you and asks if you're dead. You must tell the truth as well. No lying, and as soon as you confirm you've been murdered, the finder calls out MURDER and we switch the lights back on. Is that clear?"

Everyone nodded.

"Good." Rosamund pointed to the corner by the door. "The light switch is over there and so the person nearest the switch will have to flick it back on again. Once we can see, we must all stay where we are until the detective, that's me, tells you it's all right to move. Is everyone happy?"

There were subdued mumbles around the room.

"Come along, you can do better than that." Rosamund's face was alive with excitement. "This is going to be fun, don't spoil it ... oh, and don't forget, once the cards have been dealt, not a word to anyone about whether you have the ace or king ... and keep the cards with you so we can check later that you are indeed who you say you are."

Rosamund bounced gently on the spot as Mr Cranford took the cards and dealt them into nine piles. "No need to do any for you, my dear," he said. "If you're going to be the detective, I'd better not make you the murderer as well."

Rosamund giggled. "I hadn't thought of that. Now, everyone take a pile and then spread out. Keep the cards close to you and once we're ready, Mr Cranford will turn off the lights. While you all do that, I'll pull the fire screen closer to the flames. We don't want the escaping light giving the game away."

With his cards in his hands, Mr Cranford ambled over to the light switch. "Is everyone ready?" After receiving a murmur of assent, he flicked the switch upwards. "I must say, it's a lot quicker and easier nowadays than it was when we had the gas lamps."

Someone giggled in the darkness.

"Quiet!" Rosamund's voice was firm. "You'll give the game away. Now, everyone move around as carefully as you can. Murderer, I suggest you count to thirty to give everyone a chance to change positions. We don't want to make it too easy."

Eliza waited for those nearby to disperse and then stepped backwards towards the fire. Despite the fire screen, there were still shafts of light giving a glow to the surrounding area, but although the wind caused the flames to dance in the grate, the light failed to reach beyond the hearth. With a sigh she turned towards the centre of the room. *This has got to be the stupidest game ever invented.* She walked slowly, feeling the ground with each foot before she transferred her weight to it, willing the murderer to work quickly. Time seemed to stand still as she crept forward until eventually she turned and headed back towards the fire, only once coming close to a collision with a gentleman of unknown identity.

Once she reached the far side of the room, she paused to watch the tiny shafts of light as they burst from the sides of the fireguard. *What a shame to keep them hidden.* It was with some reluctance she turned around. *Here we go again. What is the murderer up to?* She took several steps forward but stopped abruptly. *What was that?* She strained to listen for the slightest sound but all she could hear was the wind as it swirled around the chimney and the coal as it crackled in the fireplace. After a moment, she released her breath. *It must have been a piece of coal falling in the fire.* Whatever it was, it wasn't someone shouting 'murder'. She continued on her way, but immediately a scream ripped through the darkness causing the hairs on the back of her neck to stand on end.

"Connie, is that you?" She moved as quickly as she dared towards the commotion on the other side of the room but stopped as the lights came back on.

"What on earth's the matter?" Mr Cranford stood by the

light switch as the rest of the guests gaped towards the source of the noise.

"I'm sorry." Connie's voice quivered as she spoke. "I didn't mean to stop the game, I fell over..." She glanced down at the body lying on the floor beside her. "Oh my goodness. I tripped over Rosamund."

"What on earth's she doing down there?" The smile disappeared from Mr McRae's face as he stepped forward to reach for Rosamund's hand. "Come on, up you get."

Mr Cranford chuckled. "She'll be playing a game with you."

As he spoke, Betty joined her husband. "Come along, Ros. You said you wouldn't play dead if you were accidentally murdered. We need to stop the game and start again." Betty helped Mr McRae pull her friend's hand, but when Rosamund didn't budge Betty's eyes moved to Connie. "I hope you've not hurt her."

"I didn't do it on purpose." Connie's voice was shrill as she struggled to her feet.

"Rosamund, what's up? Speak to me." Mr McRae was on his haunches.

"Stop!" Archie strode across the room and dropped to the floor beside Rosamund. "Everyone stand back. Can't you see she's injured? Rosamund, can you hear me?"

Eliza had moved to Connie's side, but stopped when she saw the handle of a metal knife protruding from Rosamund's chest. "S-she's been stabbed!"

"That wasn't me..." Connie's voice trembled as she clung to Eliza's arm.

The smile fell from Mr Cranford's face. "Rosamund! Stop this nonsense."

"Will she be all right?" Betty asked Archie as she knelt down to cradle Rosamund's head.

"I don't know. Her pulse is weak and her skin's clammy."

"Here, take these." Eliza stepped forward and offered Archie the smelling salts she carried in her handbag. "They might bring her around."

"I-is it a knife?" Connie pointed to the handle.

Archie nodded. "I would say so. In fact, it looks like one of the fruit knives from the dinner table."

"But there's not much blood."

Archie paused. "There's a bit here on the carpet, but not as much as you'd expect." He examined the wound. "Probably because the knife's still in place. The bleeding must be internal but when Mrs Appleton tripped over her, she dislodged the knife enough for a little of it to escape."

"I didn't mean to." Tears welled up in Connie's eyes. "I couldn't have known she was there."

"Of course you couldn't." Eliza put an arm around Connie's shoulder and noticed the way she was holding her wrist. "Have you hurt yourself?"

Connie nodded. "I landed on my hand."

"Come and sit down and Archie will tend to it as soon as he's free. We need to give Rosamund some space while he sees to her. Mr Cranford, perhaps the guests could have a brandy."

Mr Cranford stared down at his wife as Archie rolled her onto her back. "Brandy ... yes, right-o. I'll call the maid." He remained where he was, seemingly unable to move. "Rosamund dear, speak to me."

Eliza stayed where she was while Archie held the smelling salts under Rosamund's nose. *They're not having any effect; she's not moving.* Rosamund's skin was deathly white and an icy chill ran down Eliza's spine when the mucus collecting in Rosamund's lungs began to rattle with each laboured breath.

Eliza bundled Connie onto the nearest chair and stepped back towards the body. "Everyone, come away. She needs space. Mr McRae, will you help Betty up off the floor?"

"I'm not going anywhere." Betty drew her lips back into a snarl. "Ros is the best friend I've ever had and if she's in trouble, I'm staying with her. You deal with your friend and I'll deal with mine. None of this would have happened if it wasn't for her."

"That's not true." Tears erupted down Connie's cheeks as she stood up and stumbled back towards Eliza. "I didn't know she was on the floor. I need to get out of here; Eliza, will you come with me?"

"You're not going anywhere other than jail if you've killed her." The pitch of Betty's voice cut through the room.

"Of course I didn't kill her; she's not even dead." Connie sniffled into her handkerchief. "Eliza, tell her. I wouldn't hurt anyone. Not in real life. It's just..."

Eliza's heart sank. "It's just what?"

Connie whined as she spoke through her tears. "I was the murderer in the game. I didn't want to be, but I had the card ... the ace. I'd just pretended to kill Mrs Reed, and it was when I hurried away that I tripped over something. At first I thought it was the edge of the carpet ... how was I to know it was Rosamund?"

Eliza took hold of Connie's shaking hands and glanced at Mr Cranford. He hadn't moved since she'd asked him for the brandy and didn't look as if he was about to. Returning

Connie to the chair, she sidled over to Mr Bell, who stood by the fireplace.

"Will you go and find a maid and ask for some brandy? Mr Cranford has other things on his mind and there are a few people in here who look like they could do with one."

Mr Bell nodded and made his way to the door but stopped when he saw Mrs Reed on the settee. "Good grief, what's up with her?"

Mrs Reed was sitting down but had fallen to one side, causing her mouth to drop open.

"I've just found her like this," Mr McRae said. "I think she's fainted." He shook the older woman by the shoulders.

With one look at Mrs Reed, Eliza turned back to her father. "Sit with her while I get the smelling salts off Archie. Mr McRae, please leave her alone. Shaking her won't help."

Eliza hurried towards Archie but as she did, she saw Rosamund's arm flop from Archie's grip onto the floor.

"Oh my goodness, is she...?" She put a hand to her mouth as Archie glanced up and gave her an imperceptible nod. A moment later, he looked back down at Rosamund and ran his fingers across her eyes, closing them for the last time.

CHAPTER FIVE

The silence in the room appeared to last for an eternity but it was probably no more than a couple of seconds before the noise erupted. Jolted from her daze Eliza reached for the smelling salts and hurried back to Mr Bell.

"How is she?" She nodded at Mrs Reed.

"She's out cold, but there's a pulse, which is always a good sign."

Eliza opened the jar and held them under Mrs Reed's nose. After several breaths, she coughed and then startled everyone with a loud sneeze.

"Thank goodness for that." Mr Bell placed a hand on his heart. "I'd say she fainted when she saw Mrs Cranford."

"Rosamund?" Mrs Reed's voice was faint. "Is she going to be all right?"

Eliza paused while Archie walked towards them.

"No, Mrs Reed, I'm afraid she's not." Archie declined the seat Mr Bell had vacated for him. "Why don't you sit here and I'll get Mr Reed to join you? I think we have some brandy coming, that will help."

"Yes, that was my job." Mr Bell snapped to attention and hurried to the door. "I'll be as quick as I can."

Mr Reed crossed the room in seconds. "What's going on? Is she all right?"

"She'll be fine; just don't leave her alone." Archie gave a sad smile before he joined Eliza a little away from the group.

"Are you all right?"

Eliza closed her eyes. "I'll manage, I just can't believe it. Who would do such a thing?" She stopped and studied the guests still hovering around the body. "You do realise one of them is the murderer?"

Archie sighed. "I'm fully aware of it. Why don't you sit down while we wait for the brandy? You look as if you could do with one too."

Eliza took a seat and let her head rest on the back of the chair, momentarily closing her eyes. She opened them seconds later when Connie shook her by the shoulder.

"Eliza, tell her, I didn't do anything."

Eliza sat up with a start as Betty bore down on Connie.

"Mrs McRae, stop. What's going on? Of course Connie didn't hurt Rosamund."

"Then why was she lying on top of her body?" Betty pushed Connie on the shoulder causing the two of them to face each other.

"I told you, it was an accident. I was the murderer in the game and I'd just tapped Mrs Reed and was making my escape. I didn't know Rosamund was there, and I certainly didn't put her there."

"How do we know you're not making that up?" Mr Reed appeared more interested in their argument than his wife's well-being. "We've only got your word for it that you were the pretend murderer. Do you have the ace of spades?"

Connie patted down the outside of her skirt, her sense of urgency increasing before she put a hand in her pocket. "It's gone. I put it in here, but it must have fallen out."

"That's a fine excuse ... I expect you didn't have it in the first place."

"That's enough." Eliza stood up and held out her hands. "Connie, go and sit down. Mr Reed and Mrs McRae, you can't go around accusing someone of murder when there's no rhyme nor reason to it. Now, we know where Connie was when the body was found but we need to determine exactly where everyone else was. We'd better call the police too. Someone in this room is a murderer and we have to find out who."

"Well, it wasn't me." Betty glared at Eliza.

"Nobody's saying it was but if you want to clear your name, it would help if you co-operated." Eliza held Betty's gaze until she noticed Mr Bell return to the room with a maid following him. "Thank goodness you're here. Will you go to the police station and ask them to send someone? The rest of us need to stay here and work out what happened. I'm sure we'd all like this sorted out as soon as possible."

"Why should he go?" Mr Reed's tone forced Eliza to step back. "Why not me?"

"Mr Reed, my father is the most obvious person to send. There's no reason to suspect he had anything to do with Rosamund's death."

"There's no reason to suspect I did either..."

"I'm afraid we don't know that."

"Maybe you don't, but I do. How do I know it wasn't him?" He stabbed a finger in Mr Bell's direction.

Mr Bell stepped forward. "Of course it wasn't me. Do you think I'd try to get away with murder knowing how good a detective my daughter is?"

"That's enough." Eliza clapped her hands to quieten the noise in the room. "Can I have everyone's attention? I'm sure we're all shocked by what's just happened but I'm afraid the evidence suggests that someone in this room took Rosamund's life. We need to find out who."

There were nods of approval, but no one spoke.

"To help us, I suggest we send my father for the police. I think it's safe to assume he didn't wield the knife."

"I've told you, we don't know that..." Mr Reed thrust his face towards Eliza but she turned away.

"As you can see, not everyone in the room agrees. Is there anyone else who would rather he didn't go?" When she got no objections, she continued. "Thank you. I'd also suggest, that in the interests of time, and to help the police when they get here, we ask a few basic questions about the crime amongst ourselves."

"Why have you taken over all of a sudden?" Mr Reed asked. "Just because you were the policeman in the game, doesn't mean you have permission to carry on the pretence now. As the elder gentleman, I should be the one leading the investigation."

Eliza placed her hands on her hips while she counted to three. "I'm sorry. I wasn't aware you were familiar with police procedures. When were you last involved with a murder investigation?"

"Well, naturally I haven't been, but..."

"But you just don't want me doing it. Well, either fortunately or unfortunately, whichever way you want to look at it, I've been involved with a number of murders over the last couple of years. I don't believe anyone else has ..." She peered at each person until she noticed Archie raise an eyebrow at her.

"All right, Dr Thomson and Mrs Appleton have helped, but for now Dr Thomson needs to look at Connie's wrist, which leaves you with me. For your information, I've worked with the police four times and I'm familiar with the sort of questions they ask."

"And she's very good at it too. I'd suggest you do as she asks." Archie took his place by Connie's side and examined her wrist. "Now, if we can change the subject, I'll need some strapping. Can someone get it for me?"

"Assuming I'm allowed to leave, I'll get some on the way out." Mr Bell walked to the door but as he reached for the handle, Eliza spotted a maid standing in the corner. She had evidently finished pouring the brandy and looked frozen to the spot.

"There'll be no need for that," she said to Mr Bell. "You just get off."

Mr Bell nodded as Eliza strode towards the young girl. "Thank you, dear, leave the drinks there and we can help ourselves. I wonder if you could find us a sheet to cover the body and some strapping for Mrs Appleton's wrist."

The maid nodded furiously, her eyes wide, before she scurried from the room.

"Please, everyone help yourselves." Eliza gestured to the occasional table as she took a glass herself. "Once you have your drinks, may I ask you all to return to where you were standing when the lights were switched back on?"

"How are we supposed to remember that after everything that's happened?" Mr McRae asked.

"I know it's difficult, but could we all try? I made a mental note of everyone's positions when the light came back on and so I may be able to help if you're not sure."

"Well, if you must know, I think I was roughly in the middle of the room."

Eliza nodded. "Yes, I would say so. Possibly slightly closer to the body than that, but not much. Betty, you were close to the tree if I remember rightly, between Rosamund and Dr Thomson." She waved her arm at Archie. "I think you were nearer the window than that, yes, there. Stop. Now, Mr Cranford, you switched on the lights, but could you tell us where you were when Mrs Appleton screamed? I presume you weren't far from the light switch?"

"N-no, I don't suppose I was. I couldn't really say. I wasn't paying much attention."

"No, quite, it is difficult to work these things out in the dark. Given you reached the switch so quickly, I imagine you would have been somewhere between Rosamund and the door. Perhaps around here." Eliza stepped away from the light switch towards the middle of the room.

"Yes, that must be it." Mr Cranford took out his handkerchief and wiped his brow. "That must be it."

Eliza hesitated. *Poor man.*

"I was sitting here," Mrs Reed said from her place on the settee.

Eliza turned and gave her a solemn smile. "Of course and I think my father was nearby, if I'm not mistaken."

"He was, although I didn't realise it was him at the time. I just saw the outline of a man heading towards me. I'm sorry, I can't be much help after the lights came on. I really can't say what came over me." Mrs Reed gave a feeble smile.

"There's no need to apologise, you've had a shock, we all have. Are you feeling any better?"

"I'm as well as I can be under the circumstances, but I wonder if you'd allow us to go home."

Eliza shook her head. "I'm afraid I can't let you do that until the police arrive. I'm sure they'll want to talk to us all. Perhaps if they speak to you first, they'll let you go after that."

"Yes, thank you, dear, that would be very nice." Mrs Reed pulled her shawl more tightly around her shoulders. "That wind doesn't sound as if it's calming down and I usually like my brandy in a glass of warm milk."

"As soon as the police arrive, I'll see what I can do." Eliza turned to Mr Reed, who had reseated himself next to his wife. "Now, Mr Reed, do you remember where you were when the lights were turned back on?"

Mr Reed's hand was steady as he pointed to a spot in the centre of the room. "Rather too close to the body for my liking, but there we are. Do you need me to stand there now?"

"If you wouldn't mind; just for a moment and then you may come straight back. It might help jog someone's memory."

"So, let's see if this helps us." Eliza stepped into the middle of the room, but Mr McRae stretched an arm out in front of her.

"And where were you? You make us all stand where we were, but you've given us no hint as to your whereabouts."

Eliza took a deep breath. "No, you're right. Thank you for

reminding me." She took several steps towards the windows beyond Mr McRae and stopped. "I was about here. I believe you were to my right as we look towards the door. Does that satisfy you?"

"Well, what's one rule for us should be the same for you, that's all."

"Yes, quite. May I carry on now?" Eliza gave him a curt smile before walking gingerly towards the body. "So, Betty, Mr Reed and Mr Cranford, you were in the immediate area around Rosamund when the attack took place. Can any of you tell me whether you heard anything unusual while the lights were off?"

"No." The three of them spoke together as they shook their heads.

Eliza's brow furrowed. "So, you were all within a few feet of Rosamund and yet you heard nothing? Doesn't that strike you as odd?"

"Not really," Betty said. "With the wind howling down the chimney and the fire crackling as it was, it would be easy to miss any small sounds."

"But the fire's at the opposite end of the room. You should have been able to hear something being so far from it."

"Well, perhaps your hearing is better than mine, but it was rather loud."

"What about you two?" Eliza turned to the men. "Did the fire distract you, too?"

"I can't say I noticed." Mr Cranford shook his head. "Ros always said I never listened to her. If you must know I was thinking about the business and not paying any attention to the game. Locked in my own little world."

"Don't look at me." Mr Reed stepped back as Eliza faced

him. "I'm rather hard of hearing and didn't even notice the fire."

Eliza stared at the others, who stood further afield. "Don't tell me you all have problems with your hearing. Archie, what about you? There's nothing up with your ears; did you hear anything?"

Archie shrugged. "I'm afraid I didn't but to be honest, there might not have been much noise. Mrs Cranford clearly knew everyone in the room and so the killer could have approached her quite innocently before plunging the knife into her. There needn't have been any commotion."

"But she must have fallen to the floor."

Archie bobbed his head from side to side. "Yes, and no. She obviously ended up on the floor but if the killer was strong enough, he could easily have held her in his arms and lowered her to the ground."

"So you're saying it must have been a man?"

Archie glanced across to the still visible body. "Not necessarily. As you can see, Mrs Cranford wasn't a large lady, it would have been possible for any one of us to do it."

Eliza shuddered as she studied Rosamund again. "Where is that maid? The body really needs covering." She walked to the door just as it opened and the maid poked her head into the room. "Ah, there you are. Do you have a sheet?"

With confirmation that she did, Eliza took it from her, along with the strapping, and gave them both to Archie.

"We have to get her laid out." Mr Cranford stepped forward, but Eliza touched him on the arm to stop him.

"We will, but we'll have to leave her where she is until the police arrive. They'll want to examine the scene. Now, where were we? Ah yes, nobody heard anything. Mr McRae, you were the next closest to the incident, what about you?"

Mr McRae shrugged. "I'm really not sure. I might have heard a slight ruffle of material moments before Mrs Appleton cried out. It could have been Mrs Cranford's skirts as she fell to the floor."

"And that was immediately before we heard Mrs Appleton? That wouldn't give the killer much time to move."

"No, I don't suppose it would, unless Mrs Appleton was the killer... Not that I'm saying she is, I could be mistaken. Perhaps it was Mrs Appleton I heard falling. That might make more sense."

Eliza nodded. "Yes, it would. I must admit, I didn't notice anything, but I was one of the furthest away."

"Can I say something?" Mrs Reed had more colour in her cheeks as she leaned forward in her seat. "Mrs Appleton said she was the murderer in the game and if she was, she tapped me on the shoulder no more than five seconds before I heard her fall."

"Did you hear her trip or just her shout when she fell?"

"There was a rustle of material as Mr McRae mentioned, but Mrs Appleton hadn't touched my shoulder by then. It must have been about half a minute later that she tripped over the body."

"All right, that's interesting. So, I'd suggest that if we're looking at such a time lag between Rosamund falling and Connie tripping over her, then anyone in the room could be our killer. There would be time for everyone to move away."

"Even your father," Mr Reed snapped. "Maybe there's a reason he was so keen to leave."

Eliza pulled herself up to her full height. "That's nonsense. Archie, tell him."

When Archie appeared preoccupied with Connie's wrist, Mr Reed continued. "If it's nonsense, where is he? He should be back by now."

"He's gone to the station to report a murder, not the theft of a piece of ribbon. These things take time."

"Well, may we sit down while we wait?" Mr Reed studied his empty glass. "And get another drink? We've been through enough without you playing detective as well. I'm sure it can wait until tomorrow."

"So, the murderer has a chance to abscond?" Eliza glared at him, but her attention was distracted when the door opened and Mr Bell rejoined them.

Eliza gave Mr Reed a smug grin. "Oh good, you're here ... don't you have the police with you?"

"No." Mr Bell's shoulders sagged. "The station was busy and with it being Sunday the sergeant said he couldn't spare anyone."

"You did tell him it was a murder investigation?"

"Yes, of course I did, but he wouldn't budge until more of his men were back from their beats. He said he'd call as soon as he could."

Eliza closed her eyes and tried to relax her shoulders. "Very well. In the interests of time, I suggest we get down as many facts as we can so that once the sergeant arrives, we can pass him the information and go home. Let me get my notepad and we'll start."

CHAPTER SIX

E liza took several minutes to compose herself before she was ready to call a halt to the murmuring in the room. She was about to stand up when Archie appeared by her side.

"Are you sure you're up to this? I'll help if you want me to."

Eliza gave him a faint smile. "I'll be fine. I was just thinking, but I suppose we'd better get on with it."

Archie put a hand on her shoulder. "Don't dismiss me so quickly. I fear you'll have trouble with some of them. They're not expecting to be questioned by a woman. Maybe if I sat with you..."

Eliza got to her feet, the smile disappearing from her face. "Thank you, but it's about time they got used to it. Not that I don't want you to sit with me, but you have to let me do the talking."

"Do I ever do anything else?"

The lines on Eliza's face softened. "It has been known, but I'll say no more about it if you get everyone sitting down. I think we'd better stay around the fire, away from the body. Here, I found this; it might help."

Eliza handed him a small hand bell she'd found on one of the occasional tables.

"I'm not using that!" Archie refused to take it from her and instead clapped his hands together. "Can I have everyone's attention, please? If you could all take a seat around the fire, we'll try to get this over and done with as soon as possible."

With further grumbling, everyone wandered to the far end of the room and found a seat.

Eliza stood by the fireplace as she waited for them. "Right, thank you. I'm afraid this isn't going to be easy, but we need to find out who took the life of dear Rosamund. The biggest question I have, and it must be troubling you too, is who would want Rosamund dead? I only met her earlier today but from what I saw and what you've told me, she was very popular. Not the sort of person you'd expect to make enemies. Can anyone think of a reason why someone would want to kill her?" When the room remained silent, Eliza turned to Mr Cranford. "What about you, sir? As the victim's husband have you any ideas?"

Mr Cranford's watery eyes stared blankly at her. "Me? Well, no, I can't say I have."

Eliza glanced at Betty, wondering if perhaps she knew any better, but when Betty did nothing but stare at the carpet, Eliza turned back to Mr Cranford. "Do you know if she'd upset anyone recently?"

"Rosamund upset someone?" Mr Cranford gave an involuntary laugh. "No, of course not. She was such a delight..."

"What about you, Betty? You and Rosamund were very close I believe."

Betty didn't look up. "We were when she wanted to be. What good is she to me now? She knew I couldn't manage without her and yet she does this…"

Eliza's mouth dropped open, and she glanced at Archie before she continued. "You can't think she did this on purpose?"

"Well, she only has herself to blame. She was the one who insisted we play this silly game. I told her it wasn't necessary, but she loved being the centre of attention."

"And so she'd mentioned it in advance?"

Betty's head shot up. "No. I found out about it at the same time as you, but I told her what I thought. I said you'd all prefer to go home. If she'd listened to me…"

Eliza paused. "All right, let's consider that for a moment. Had Rosamund told anyone she was planning a game of Murder in the Dark today? Mr Cranford, had she mentioned it to you?"

The expression on Mr Cranford's face didn't change as he stared blankly at Eliza. "I hadn't seen much of her…"

"She hadn't said anything in the days leading up to the luncheon? She must have spoken to you about Christmas."

Mr Cranford shook his head. "No…"

"Mr Cranford's been very busy at work lately," Betty said. "He and Rosamund hadn't spoken properly for weeks. That's right, isn't it, Mr Cranford?"

This time he nodded. "Yes."

Eliza turned back to Betty. "And so you saw more of Rosamund than anyone else and yet she hadn't told you of her plans?"

"I've already told you."

Eliza sighed. "All right, so we've established that everyone was fond of Rosamund, nobody knew about the game until we were finishing luncheon and everyone in the room had the opportunity to wield the knife. That doesn't give us much to go on."

"I think we should check everyone for signs of blood," Mr Reed said. "Whoever stabbed poor Rosamund must have some on their hands or clothes."

Archie stretched out his hands for everyone to see. "We could, but to be honest there wasn't much. The killer plunged the knife in in such a way that there was very little blood. I imagine Mrs Appleton will have some on her because she probably knocked the handle, but other than that you can see by the wound, there's not a lot of blood."

Eliza sensed the tension in the room rising again. "Why don't we check, anyway? It can't do any harm."

With Archie tasked with examining the clothes and hands of the men, Eliza ran her eyes over the ladies.

"Check handkerchiefs too," Eliza said. "If anyone had blood on their hands, that would be an obvious place to wipe it. Now, let me look at you, Connie. Oh dear, what's that?" She pointed to a wet patch on Connie's navy skirt. "It's a good job your skirt's dark...

"It's ruined!"

"Don't be silly. I don't suppose it will stain. A good scrub should get it out; the skirt's new, isn't it?"

Connie sniffed. "It was, but I won't be wearing it again. Even if there's no mark, I'll know..."

"She can't go washing it, anyway. The police need it as

evidence." Betty studied the skirt. "If you ask me, that's not the mark of someone who fell onto some blood, it looks more like the blood has dripped onto them."

"Nonsense," Eliza said. "You can tell it's been smudged. Now, what about you?"

"I don't have anything on me." Betty's light grey skirt appeared pristine even as Eliza straightened out the folds.

"No, that looks clear." After checking Betty's hands and handkerchief, Eliza moved to Mrs Reed.

"Now then, Mrs Reed, there's no need to be nervous."

"It wasn't me though, honestly, I couldn't say how this got here."

Eliza stared down at the right-hand side of Mrs Reed's emerald green skirt.

"Blood!"

"I didn't do it." Mrs Reed's voice was an octave higher than it had been moments earlier. "I only noticed it when you started to talk about it."

Eliza indicated to Archie to come and check the mark for himself.

"It looks like something that was covered in blood has been wiped onto your skirt. Can I see your hands?"

Mrs Reed's hands shook as she held them out for the doctor.

"What's going on here?" Mr Reed jostled Eliza out of the way.

"We're not sure yet." Archie indicated that Mrs Reed could put her hands back on her lap. "Your wife has blood on her skirt and we can't say how it got there. Her hands are clean enough, which suggests that someone else wiped it onto her. Mrs Reed, do you remember feeling anyone brushing against you?"

"Well … n-no. Nobody except Mrs Appleton when she pretended to murder me."

"Me!" Connie instinctively held out her hands. "It wasn't me; I don't have any marks on my hands. Eliza, you've already seen them …. and Dr Thomson has."

"Calm down." Eliza put a hand on Connie's arm. "If you were our pretend murderer, I presume you touched Mrs Reed's shoulder before you fell."

Connie visibly relaxed. "Yes, I did … of course I did."

Archie crouched down beside Mrs Reed. "Please think, do you remember anyone touching you after we heard Mrs Appleton fall?"

"I-I couldn't say, but I don't think so. As you know, I was sitting down when the lights came on and then, well, once I saw Rosamund, I fainted. When I recovered, Mr Bell was with me."

"I knew he had something to do with it," Mr Reed said.

Mr Bell jumped to his feet. "Don't go blaming me."

"Well, who else is there to blame?"

Archie stood between the two men. "Mr Bell has no blood on his hands or clothes."

"But he went out, didn't he? He could have washed his hands easily enough."

"If I'd have been the murderer, do you think I'd have come back?"

"Exactly!" Eliza said. "Father was watching over your wife, not setting her up for murder."

Mr Reed's eyes glinted as he stared at Connie. "But your

friend wasn't. She was in the chair next to my wife; I saw her myself."

Betty glared at Eliza. "Of course. Isn't it obvious? Your friend murdered my dear Rosamund and when she found the blood on her, she wiped it on poor Mrs Reed, hoping that no one was looking."

"No, that's not true..." Connie's eyes were moist as she stared at Eliza. "Why would I? Eliza, you always say that people need a motive as well as the opportunity. I had no reason to want Rosamund dead."

"You were jealous of her." There was venom in Betty's voice. "She was so nice, and you hated her for it."

"That's enough, Mrs McRae." Archie stepped between her and Connie. "Mr McRae, could you come and sit with your wife, please? I think things are getting a little out of hand and we all need to calm down."

Mr McRae's face was unreadable as Eliza stepped back and allowed him to take the seat beside Betty.

"Let me see if I can get us all a nice cup of tea..." Eliza turned on her heel and hurried to the door.

"And some more brandy," Mr Reed called after her.

Before she could cross the room, there was a knock at the front door. She hurried into the hallway to see a short, stocky man, with a large handlebar moustache, step into the house. His navy blue uniform with three stripes on the arm confirmed he was from the police. *Thank goodness for that.*

"Good evening, Sergeant. Thank you for coming." She headed down the hall with a polite smile fixed on her lips. "Forgive me for being forward but we've been waiting for you. My name's Mrs Thomson, and I've already started the questioning, but things are getting rather tense..."

"*You* have?" The sergeant took a step back.

"Now, don't be like that, Sergeant. I can assure you, I've plenty of experience. Shall I update you on what we've found out so far?"

"If you don't mind, the first thing I want to do is find out what's been going on. Who's the man of the house here?"

"Well, that would be Mr Cranford, but he's in no fit state to give you all the details."

"I'll be the judge of that, thank you. If you could just take me to him, that will be all."

"Y-yes, of course, but may I suggest that if you have any questions, you ask me?"

"I'll do no such thing." The sergeant set off down the hall causing Eliza to scurry after him. As soon as he stepped into the drawing room he stopped abruptly, his eyes fixed on the shape under the sheet.

"I'm afraid that's poor Mrs Cranford," Eliza said. "We left her there so you could study the scene yourself."

"Yes, quite." He glanced at the body before striding to the far end of the room. "Which of you gentlemen is Mr Cranford?"

Mr Cranford stood up and offered the sergeant his hand. "Good evening, Sergeant..."

"Dixon, sir. Sergeant Dixon. I'm sorry to hear about your wife, but I'll need to ask you about the events of this afternoon. Is there somewhere quiet we can go?"

"Well, yes, but you might be better speaking to the others first."

"In good time, sir. The first thing is to speak to you and get a doctor here to give us more details about the death."

Archie stood up and offered his hand to the sergeant. "Good evening, Sergeant. I'm Dr Thomson."

"Dr *Thomson*?"

A faint smile crossed Archie's lips. "Yes, I see you've already met my wife."

The sergeant glanced at Eliza. "Yes, indeed."

"Don't worry, she's quite respectable. I can vouch for her."

Eliza opened her mouth to respond when a raised eyebrow from Archie forced her to close it again.

"I've already examined the body and can tell you the victim was stabbed with what I believe to be a fruit knife," Archie said. "There was very little visible blood, but I suspect the patient had internal bleeding and died of shock. We'll need a post-mortem to confirm that obviously."

"Were you summoned to the house to treat the patient?"

"No, in actual fact we were guests for luncheon and were here when the murder took place."

"Now, sir, let's not be hasty," Sergeant Dixon said. "We don't know it was murder."

Eliza gasped as she stepped between the sergeant and her husband. "What else could it be when there's a corpse with a knife in its chest? It was hardly an accident."

The sergeant held up his hand. "Mrs Thomson, as I told you, this is police business now. I need to talk to Mr Cranford first and then I'll speak to Dr Thomson. I don't want to jump to any conclusions."

"We've already been through that while we waited for you. If you'd just let me tell you what we know…"

The sergeant turned his back on Eliza as he focussed on Mr Cranford. "Is there another room we may use, sir, somewhere we won't be disturbed?"

"Well, yes, the morning room isn't being used. Follow me."

As the two of them left the room, Eliza bristled under the sergeant's glare. He could do that all he liked. He'd soon realise he needed her help if he wanted to get this case solved before Christmas.

CHAPTER SEVEN

A s soon as Mr Cranford led the sergeant from the room Eliza and Connie moved from the fireside to sit on a settee closer to the door. Within seconds Archie and Mr Bell joined them.

"What a to-do this is," Mr Bell said. "I wouldn't like to be the police trying to sort this one out. We're all friends here, I can't imagine why anyone would have harmed poor Mrs Cranford."

"Is that what you'll say to Sergeant Dixon?" Eliza asked.

"Probably. What else can I say? I didn't see or hear anything."

"What about you, Archie? What will you tell the sergeant?"

Archie shrugged. "Nothing you don't know already. That Mrs Cranford was still alive when we found her but died shortly afterwards. I'll show him the body and the murder weapon."

"Yes, I suppose you'll have to ... although don't be surprised if he decides she accidentally fell on the knife."

"Don't be like that, he hasn't seen the injury yet."

"Well, he shouldn't jump to conclusions then. At the very least, he could have taken our word for it."

"Don't take it personally." Archie patted Eliza on the back of a hand. "He will by the time I've finished with him."

Eliza nodded. "Good. I imagine he'll ask you about the time of the stabbing. What will you say?"

Archie puffed out his cheeks. "It could have been any time after the lights were switched off. Did anyone notice what time that was?"

"It was half past three when we came back in here," Connie said. "We then spent quite a while talking about the rules of the game and dealing the cards. It was probably at least quarter to four, I would say."

"I wouldn't argue with that," Eliza said. "She must have been stabbed shortly after the lights went out, because we didn't play for long. And then at best I imagine she only lived two or three minutes after she was attacked."

Mr Bell leaned forward and put his head in his hands.

"Are you all right?" Archie asked.

"I think I'm still in shock. I can't quite believe it, such a lovely woman. We should be at home by now planning what we're doing this week, not sitting here."

Eliza gripped her father's hand. "We'll find the killer as soon as we can. We just need to get Sergeant Dixon to accept help."

Eliza glanced up as the drawing room door opened and the sergeant walked back in ahead of Mr Cranford.

"Ah, Dr Thomson, there you are. I'll speak to you next and then speak to the ladies after that."

Archie stood up. "Certainly, Sergeant. Perhaps I should show you the body first."

Eliza didn't take her eyes off Archie as he crouched down beside the sheet, discreetly lifted a corner and pointed to the stab wound. She waited for them to leave the room before she crept forward and lifted the sheet herself.

"What are you doing?" Connie appeared by her side. "You really shouldn't be touching the body."

"I won't touch it, but I wanted to check something."

Connie bent down as Eliza pointed to Rosamund's mouth. "See this reddening? It's only faint, but I didn't notice it earlier. It suggests that the murderer had a hand over her mouth when they stabbed her, although the fact that the mark isn't more prominent suggests there was no struggle."

Connie nodded. "That would explain why nobody heard anything. Do you think Dr Thomson noticed it?"

"I'm not sure. I was watching them, and Archie seemed more concerned with the stab wound."

"You should have said something."

"And upset the sergeant even more?" Eliza placed a hand on her heart. "As if I'd do that."

"Oi, what are you two doing over there?" Mr Reed strode towards them.

"Nothing." Eliza straightened the sheet and hurried to her feet. "The body hadn't been properly covered after the sergeant looked at it. I was just tidying it up. We really need to get the undertaker here now the sergeant's seen it."

"They won't be available on a Sunday evening."

"No, I'm aware of that. Perhaps we should move the body ourselves. I'll mention it to Dr Thomson when he gets back. We'd better not do anything on our own."

Mr Reed nodded and wandered back to his seat as Eliza and Connie rejoined Mr Bell.

"You don't think the sergeant will blame me, do you?" Connie asked. "I promise I had the ace, but I can't find it anywhere. I have the other cards, look." She produced four playing cards from her pocket. "Why would the one I need be the one that's missing?"

Eliza shrugged. "Isn't it always the way? You probably wanted to keep it safe and put it somewhere else."

Connie's forehead puckered. "I'm sure I didn't. I just hope the fact that I don't have it doesn't incriminate me."

"Stop worrying, it takes a lot more evidence than that to accuse someone. You were just unfortunate. It could have been any one of us who tripped over the body."

Connie didn't look convinced. "I hope Sergeant Dixon sees it like that. I know some of these policemen take the easy option ... and that would be me. You will stick up for me, won't you?"

"Of course I will."

Mr Bell nodded. "We all will."

All conversation stopped as the door opened and the sergeant led Dr Thomson back into the room.

"I need everyone to stay in here. No exceptions," he said to Archie.

"Don't worry. I'll make sure nobody goes out."

With a nod, the sergeant addressed the room. "Did you all hear that? I don't want anyone coming or going without my express permission. In the absence of a constable, Dr Thomson has agreed to keep watch for me. Is that clear?" Sergeant Dixon waited until they all nodded. "Good."

"Who would you like to see next?" Archie asked.

"Perhaps it should be me." Eliza was on her feet.

"No. I don't think so, Mrs Thomson. I'd like to speak to Mrs McRae next. She was Mrs Cranford's friend, I believe."

Eliza scowled at the sergeant as he led Betty from the room.

"Sit down." Archie tugged on her hand, but she stood firm. "There's no point upsetting yourself. Not every police officer will let you help them with their enquiries."

"But he doesn't know anything about what's happened."

"Stop worrying. I told him everything we know, which if we're being honest isn't very much."

"But will he ask the right questions?"

"Eliza, stop. You're not the only one who's ever solved a murder. This is what he gets paid to do."

"Goodness knows what Betty will tell him," Connie said, as Eliza slumped back into her chair. "She'd like to pin the blame on me, that's for sure, although I've no idea why. She was hardly likely to kill Rosamund herself."

Eliza sat up straight. "Or was she? If Betty didn't do it why does she want to blame you? Could she have killed her?" Eliza turned to Archie. "Perhaps she was angry with Rosamund for talking to us and ignoring her."

"You can't go blaming her without evidence," Archie said.

"Eliza has a point though," Mr Bell said. "Mrs McRae's been quite hysterical since the murder. Have you seen the look in her eyes? She may not have meant to kill Rosamund, but perhaps she couldn't help herself."

"I don't know," Archie said. "Judging by the way she's behaved today, I'd say she was more likely to stab her husband than Mrs Cranford."

"You've noticed that too?" Eliza asked. "I must admit,

there's been something strange going on. I don't think they've said two words to each other since we arrived ... other than when Mr McRae had to calm her down."

Betty's shrill voice suddenly pierced the air and Eliza turned to see her standing by the door pointing at Connie. "There she is, Sergeant."

"Me! What about me?" Connie's voice squeaked.

"Look at her skirt. It's covered in blood. She's the one you want, I'm telling you."

"Given that Mrs Appleton tripped and landed on the body, it's hardly surprising she has blood on her skirt," Eliza said. "It doesn't prove she wielded the knife."

"I told you her friend would stick up for her, didn't I?" The pitch of Betty's voice continued to rise. "She's been so busy playing detective, trying to accuse everyone else. Well, I think you ought to look here first."

"Thank you, Mrs McRae, that will be all." The sergeant half pushed, half guided Betty back to the chair she'd left by the fireplace. "Mrs Appleton, if you wouldn't mind joining me in the other room."

Eliza was on her feet. "I'm coming with her."

The sergeant's glare forced Eliza back into her seat. "Mrs Thomson, when I want to see you, I'll ask, but at the moment I wish to speak to Mrs Appleton on her own." He took hold of Connie's arm. "This way, madam."

"I'm going to have a word with her." Eliza glowered at Betty as she stood up but Archie pulled her back down.

"Stay where you are; you'll only make things worse."

"I can't let her get away with accusing Connie."

"Just sit there for a moment and look at her." Archie nodded in the direction of Betty. She was sitting with the

Reeds, while Mr McRae sat on the other side of the fireplace with Mr Cranford. She didn't appear to be part of either group and Mr McRae was acting as if she wasn't there at all. "Mr Bell, how often do you see Mr and Mrs McRae together?"

Mr Bell's forehead creased. "Well, I see them in church most weeks but now you come to mention it, it's rarely just the two of them. Betty is always with Rosamund and Mr McRae is usually with one or other of the gentlemen."

Eliza cocked her head to one side. "That's interesting. Did you ever see Betty talking to anyone other than Rosamund?"

"I can't say I did, not without Rosamund being with her."

"So, if Mr and Mrs McRae aren't seeing eye to eye, and Rosamund was Betty's only friend, she's going to miss her more than most. Why would she kill her?"

"We don't know she did," Archie said.

"But if it wasn't her, why try to pin the blame on Connie? She doesn't look as if she's trying to defend anyone else."

Archie shrugged. "Maybe she's just good at hiding it. She's not likely to come in here and talk about it."

"I suppose not but we need to ask what she's up to. I know she's upset, but that's no reason to accuse someone else without any evidence."

Eliza flicked open her notebook. "Archie, you were closest to Betty when the lights came back on; did you notice anything unusual about her? Did she seem more flustered than she had been over luncheon?"

Archie laughed. "How could she have been any more flustered? You saw yourself she's been hysterical most of the afternoon."

"That's as may be, but..." Eliza flinched as the door flew

open and Connie hurried in, tears streaming down her cheeks.

"He thinks it's me." Connie pointed to Betty. "He believes *her*."

"Is that true?" Eliza stood up and faced the sergeant as he followed Connie into the room.

"I'm keeping all lines of investigation open at the moment. Until I've spoken to everyone, I'm in no position to say anything."

"But you're..."

"Please, Mrs Thomson, will you stop trying to tell me how to do my job? Now, if you'll excuse me, I need to speak to Mrs Reed next."

Ignoring Eliza's protests, he made his way to the far end of the room.

"I'd like to accompany my wife, if I may." Mr Reed spoke as the sergeant helped Mrs Reed to her feet. "This whole episode has been very upsetting for her and I won't leave her on her own."

Sergeant Dixon smiled. "Yes, of course, sir. Walk this way."

"Why is he allowed to sit in with Mrs Reed when I couldn't accompany Connie?" Eliza spoke to no one in particular but loud enough for everyone to hear.

"Eliza, will you calm down?" Archie's voice was gruff. "He said he would speak to the ladies first, which means it'll be your turn next. Just sit quietly for a few minutes and think of what you'd like to say."

"I've already decided what I'm going to say..."

"Well, do it in such a way that he doesn't want to lock you up afterwards."

Eliza sat back in her chair and counted to ten. *I bet this fellow's never investigated a murder in his life. He's no idea what he's doing if he thinks Connie's the culprit. I'll tell him...*

By the time the sergeant returned to the room, Eliza's breathing had calmed.

"Right, Mrs Thomson, let's get this done with before I speak to the gentlemen."

"Get this done with! Sergeant, have you any idea...?" A look from Archie forced her to take a deep breath. *All right, I'll be on my best behaviour.*

CHAPTER EIGHT

The sergeant had clearly made himself comfortable in the morning room. The small rectangular table had been pulled into the centre of the room and the sergeant sat in an upholstered chair in front of the fire. He indicated for Eliza to sit opposite him on one of the wooden dining chairs. Compared to the drawing room, it was warm and Eliza dropped her shawl from her shoulders as she sat down.

"Now, Mrs Thomson," he started, "you were obviously in the room when the murder took place. Can you tell me what you were doing at the time of the incident?"

Eliza sat up straight with her hands on her knees. "As we were playing a game of Murder in the Dark, I was wandering aimlessly around the drawing room."

"Yes, I appreciate that, but could you be more specific about your whereabouts?"

"Unfortunately, I can't, and I would suggest that nobody else in the room should have been able to either. If they've told you otherwise, I'm afraid they were lying because the room was almost pitch-black. What I can tell you, though, is where I was when the lights were switched back on."

"And where was that?"

Eliza produced a piece of notepaper from her bag and placed it on the table, jabbing her finger in the centre. "Approximately here. As you can see, I was close to Mr McRae, but not as close to the body as Mr Reed or Mrs McRae." She stabbed at each name on the paper as she spoke.

The sergeant copied the image into his notebook. "And you collected this information at the time of the murder?"

"More or less. When we heard Mrs Appleton call out, Mr Cranford switched on the lights and we saw that she had fallen over someone. We didn't realise what had happened straight away, or even the extent of Mrs Cranford's injuries, but I made a rough note of where everyone was standing, which is how I produced this."

"Why would you do that?" The sergeant's forehead creased.

"Because Mrs Cranford wanted me to help her be the detective in the game. I needed to be prepared, but once we realised the severity of the situation, it became even more important. While we were waiting for you to arrive, we confirmed everyone's positions, which is what you see here."

The sergeant gave the paper a final glance before returning to his notebook. "How well did you know Mrs Cranford?"

"Not well at all; we only met earlier today. She wanted to hear about the murder investigations I'd been involved with."

Sergeant Dixon appeared unimpressed. "And because you think you have the skills of Sherlock Holmes, you took it upon yourself to lead the questioning this afternoon."

Eliza flinched. "I wouldn't put it like that, but I do have experience..."

"And I understand you're particularly friendly with Mrs Appleton."

"Yes, we've known each other for many years and she's my next-door neighbour."

"And so it isn't unexpected that you refuse to acknowledge she could be the murderer."

Eliza took a deep breath. "Sergeant, I know Mrs Appleton isn't the murderer, because she would never do anything to hurt anyone. Even if she disliked someone, she wouldn't dream of killing them. Why would she plunge a knife into the chest of a woman she had only just met?"

"Are you sure about that?" Sergeant Dixon stared at Eliza. "Can you confirm with certainty that they hadn't met at some point in the past and there was a score to settle?"

"This is nonsense..."

"I'm afraid it's not, Mrs Thomson. Mrs Appleton was on top of the body when the lights were switched on and had blood on her skirt. A little too convenient to say she tripped, don't you think?"

"No, I don't." Eliza strained to keep her voice steady. "It was a terrible shock for her and she sprained her wrist into the bargain. Did you notice the blood on Mrs Reed's skirt? There's less of an explanation for that than there is for the stain on Mrs Appleton's skirt, and we need to find out how it got there."

The sergeant made a note in his book. "Mrs Reed was sitting quietly on the settee when the murder happened; we can hardly accuse her."

"Sergeant, I hope you're not going to continue with this line of thinking because if you are, you'll leave me no choice but to contact Inspector Adams, an acquaintance of mine from New Scotland Yard. He'll vouch for the fact that Mrs Appleton would do no such thing and he won't take kindly to another suspect being eliminated from the enquiry quite so easily."

A smirk spread across the sergeant's face. "Mrs Thomson, I'm sure this inspector of yours has better things to do than settle petty squabbles."

"Accusing my friend of murder is not some petty squabble and if you think Inspector Adams won't call to sort out your mess, then I suggest you speak to my father, Mr Bell. He happens to be on good terms with him too."

"Your father knows him?"

"Yes, and for your information, I've helped the inspector with several investigations over the last couple of years. Now, if you don't want me to trouble him, I'd advise you to wipe that smile off your face and consider who the real murderer is and what their motive could be. Everyone in the room had the opportunity to plunge the knife into poor Mrs Cranford but not all of us had a motive."

"We don't know that."

Eliza took a deep breath. "You might not, but let's put that to one side for now. Did you find out anything of any significance from the people you've already spoken to? What about Mr Cranford? Husbands are often guilty of murdering their wives. Did you sense any motive he may have had?"

The sergeant shook his head. "The man was too upset; I couldn't get a word out of him."

"Maybe that's because he's the killer. Did you think of that? It might have seemed like a good idea at the time, but once Mrs Cranford was dead, and he realised what he'd done, he could have become racked with guilt. He wouldn't be the first man to find himself in such a situation."

"Mrs Thomson, that's a preposterous suggestion. Mr and Mrs Cranford were regular churchgoers, and the man is overcome with grief..."

Eliza sighed. "Going to church doesn't exonerate him. I'm sure most convicted killers have been to church at some point in their lives. What about Mr and Mrs Reed? You saw them together despite the fact you refused to let me join Mrs Appleton."

"A man has a duty to care for his wife. Of course I let him join her."

"Unfortunately, Mrs Appleton no longer has a husband to care for her, but she needed someone with her just as much as Mrs Reed did."

Sergeant Dixon straightened his back and pulled himself up to his full height. "I won't deny a man who wants to help his wife. If Dr Thomson had wanted to join you, or if he'd offered to escort Mrs Appleton, then I wouldn't have objected."

"Oh, that's all right then." Eliza couldn't keep the sarcasm from her voice.

"Mrs Thomson, that's enough. Mrs Reed was terribly upset. She'd fainted when the body was found and was still unsteady on her feet. Would you deny her assistance?"

"No, of course not." *There's no point arguing, I'm not going to win. Count to three.* "So, did you find out anything of interest from her?"

"She said she'd felt a tap on the shoulder during the game and so had sat on a settee pretending to be dead. There was a man nearby who was about to come to her aid and she found out later it was Mr Bell. I've no reason to doubt her and it's highly unlikely she'd be able to inflict such a wound."

"And so you're happy to ignore the blood on her skirt? Someone put it there."

The sergeant squirmed in his seat before studying his notes.

"All right, what about Mr Reed?" Eliza said. "His movements are less certain. He was close to the body when the lights came back on, but I haven't established whether he had a good relationship with Mrs Cranford, other than the fact they were neighbours."

Sergeant Dixon shrugged. "Mr Reed was more concerned for his wife than for himself. She's had a nasty shock, and I promised they could go home as soon as the interviews were over."

Eliza's forehead furrowed. "Are you sure that was wise? We've no idea about Mr Reed's background and he's been hostile to any investigation all afternoon. Mrs Reed may not have committed the murder, but she could be providing a good reason for her husband to get away from the scene of the crime. We can't just let them walk out of here without having a firmer grasp of who the culprit might be."

"That will be for me to decide."

Eliza paused and took a deep breath. "Naturally. All I'm saying is we need to keep an eye on him." She turned back to her notes. "What about Mrs McRae? You spoke to her alone and I get the distinct impression that your suspicions about

Mrs Appleton are as a direct result of your conversation with her."

"Mrs McRae was hardly likely to murder her best friend. She was very tearful and told me that she and Mrs Cranford were as close as sisters. She'll miss her dreadfully."

"But did she tell you she was jealous of the attention Mrs Cranford was giving me earlier today? Mrs McRae was used to having all that affection to herself, but suddenly Mrs Cranford was ignoring her. I've been watching her all afternoon and I would say that she's rather angry. Whether she was furious enough to kill her friend and blame it on someone else, though, is difficult to know."

"She was adamant that Mrs Appleton must be the killer."

"And did she provide any evidence, other than the fact that Mrs Appleton fell over the body?"

The sergeant's cheeks coloured. "No."

"So she's made an enemy of Mrs Appleton for reasons known only to herself and she's already at odds with Mr McRae. I would say they'd had an argument before they arrived here today. They haven't acknowledged each other this afternoon except for a brief two-minute spell when Mrs McRae was upset and Mr McRae had to deal with her. Did she mention anything about that?"

"Of course she didn't. That's personal information; there was no reason for it to come up."

Eliza sighed. "If you'll forgive me for saying, that's what you're missing in this inquiry. Perhaps if you'd let me sit in while you were questioning her, I could have asked. It worked well enough when I sat in with Inspector Adams. I'd ask the questions he couldn't."

"As I said, this is a police investigation and I'll conduct things my own way."

"Well, may I suggest that when you speak to Mr McRae, you ask him about the argument? There's something going on that I suspect could be relevant."

"What happens between husband and wife is of no concern to the police. Now, if that's all…"

Eliza stood up and paced the room. "No, actually, it's not all. I hate to be troublesome, but this is a murder investigation and we have to work out who had a reason to kill their hostess. From where I was standing, Mrs McRae appeared furious rather than shocked when the body was discovered. She certainly didn't look as upset as you might imagine. You'll have heard that Mrs Cranford was still alive when we found her. Could that explain Mrs McRae's reaction? I would say you need to speak to her again and this time focus on what she was doing, instead of listening to her accusing Mrs Appleton."

The sergeant shifted in his seat. "I'm sure that won't be necessary."

Eliza walked back to the table and placed both hands on it. "Sergeant Dixon, we haven't seen eye to eye so far this afternoon, but all I want to do is help. It's Christmas in three days' time and I'm sure you'd like the suspect behind bars by then. I imagine Mrs Dixon has all the arrangements in hand for your Christmas. What will you have to eat? Goose, perhaps. And I bet she's been baking every day for the last month to get the plum pudding and other treats prepared. She won't be happy if you're interviewing suspects on Christmas Day. I don't suppose you'd like it either."

The sergeant licked his lips as he stared at Eliza.

"If you'd let me help, you could be at home in front of the

fire by the time the final preparations are being made. I've a list of questions that need answering and I can run through them with you if you like?"

For the first time that afternoon, the sergeant nodded. "Very well."

CHAPTER NINE

Eliza allowed herself a smile as Sergeant Dixon read the questions she'd given him, but it quickly turned to a frown when he pushed the paper towards her and leaned back in his chair.

"Where do you get such fanciful ideas? This should be a simple case of arresting the person closest to the body and you've turned it into a web of suspicion."

"I'm sorry, Sergeant, but you need more than that to arrest someone for murder. You have to establish a motive and this is the only way we can do that. It's never easy asking some of those questions, but that's where I could help. If Inspector Adams was happy for me to sit in..."

The sergeant sighed. "I really don't know..."

Eliza studied the notes that now stared up at her from the table. "I'll tell you what, why don't you interview my father next? He won't mind if I'm here and then you'll see if you're comfortable with me helping. If you're not, then I'll go."

After another pause, the sergeant reluctantly nodded his head. "Very well then; let me get him."

While she waited, Eliza vacated the seat intended for the suspects and positioned a high-backed dining chair to the right-hand side of the sergeant. *I might as well do things properly.*

"Do you mind your daughter sitting in with us?" Sergeant Dixon asked Mr Bell as they returned to the morning room.

Mr Bell winked at Eliza. "Not at all, Sergeant. I happen to know she's rather good at this."

"Are you familiar with this Inspector Adams she claims to have helped?"

Mr Bell shuddered. "I most certainly am. Without him and my daughter I might not be sitting here now. The two of them make an excellent pair of detectives if you ask me."

Eliza couldn't fathom the expression on Sergeant Dixon's face. Was it disbelief, incredulity, admiration? *No, not admiration.*

"Right, well, good. Shall we start? Now, going back to the events of this afternoon, I understand you were close to Mrs Reed when Mrs Cranford's body was found."

"That's right, and to save you asking, I didn't see or hear anything unusual leading up to the incident."

The sergeant's pencil scratched on the paper of his notebook as he wrote. "Can you prove the murder was nothing to do with you?"

Mr Bell shrugged. "Not directly, but I'll tell you this, I wouldn't be sat here now if it was. I'd have disappeared rather quickly instead of coming to fetch you. The fact that I reported the incident and came straight back should be proof enough that I've nothing to hide."

Sergeant Dixon nodded. "Did you know Mrs Cranford well?"

"Not really, although she was a good neighbour. She always kept an eye on the local houses and regularly checked up on everyone to makc sure we were all safe. She'd do shopping for those who couldn't get out and spent a lot of time at church. I don't remember anyone with a bad word to say about her."

Eliza tentatively put her hand in the air. "Would you mind if I interrupted?" Eliza waited for permission before speaking to her father. "What about her relationship with the neighbours here today? Had it not been for us, Mrs McRae could have had Mrs Cranford to herself. Did she spend much time with Mr and Mrs Reed or were they just here to make up the numbers?"

"Gosh, no, nothing like that. They were best of friends. Mrs Cranford once told me she treated them as if they were her parents ... she'd apparently lost her own when she was young."

"Didn't they have children of their own?"

Mr Bell shook his head. "Not that I'm aware of."

The sergeant turned to Eliza. "Are you suggesting that if they had a good relationship with Mrs Cranford, neither of them would have wanted her dead?"

"Perhaps, unless they'd argued over something. Not that I'm saying they had, we just need to keep our eyes and ears open in case they say anything."

"I can do that from next door," Mr Bell said. "I get along well enough with Mr Reed, or at least I did until today; why don't I go and sit with them?"

"Yes, you do that." Eliza gave the sergeant a sideways glance. "I'm hoping Sergeant Dixon will let me stay here while he interviews Mr McRae. I can't help thinking he knows more than he's told us." Eliza hadn't realised she was holding her breath until the sergeant nodded. "Thank you, I'll make sure you don't regret it."

"Have you finished with me then, Sergeant?" Mr Bell asked.

"Yes, for now, but you must come and tell me if you find out any more from Mr Reed."

Without further comment, the sergeant escorted Mr Bell back to the drawing room. It was several minutes later when he returned with Mr McRae and Eliza let out an involuntary gasp. His eyes were red and swollen, and his previously neat hair was dishevelled. *Oh my goodness, he's been crying.* He stared at Eliza but said nothing as he sat down.

"Now, Mr McRae," the sergeant started, "you were standing in the middle of the room when the lights were switched back on. Did you see or hear anything?"

Mr McRae clenched his fists in his lap. "Nothing of any importance it seems." He spat out his words. "I wish I had; I'd give that villain what for."

"I'm sure there's no need for that, we don't want any more bodies. Have you any idea why someone would want Mrs Cranford dead?"

Mr McRae fought back his tears as he took a handkerchief from his pocket. "I can't imagine why anyone in London would want her dead, let alone someone in this house. If I hadn't been there to see it with my own eyes, I wouldn't have believed it."

"Yes, right." The sergeant studied his notebook before turning to Eliza. "Mrs Thomson, you had a question."

"I did, thank you. Mr McRae, I was standing beside you when the lights came back on and I've been thinking about your reaction. It was rather unusual. You didn't wait for your eyes to adjust to the light but instead you rushed straight to Mrs Cranford's body; I don't think anyone else had even noticed her. I can't put my finger on it, but it was as if you were expecting her to be exactly where she was."

Mr McRae's jaw tightened. "Don't be ridiculous, how would I know that?"

"That's what I'm trying to work out." Eliza cocked her head to one side as she stared at him.

"All right, I won't deny that I looked for her as soon as the lights came back on." Mr McRae squirmed in his seat. "She'd been so excited to be the detective and I wanted to see the look on her face when she spotted the victim. It was a coincidence that I saw her straight away."

"You were looking for her on the floor?"

Mr McRae gave her a steely-eyed glare. "Of course I wasn't, I just saw her before anyone else, that's all."

Sergeant Dixon interrupted. "How well did you know Mrs Cranford?"

Mr McRae glanced down at his hands. "Not as well as Betty obviously, but Ros and Mr Cranford would often join us for dinner, or we'd come here. She was a good neighbour ... as is Mr Cranford."

Eliza softened her expression and held Mr McRae's gaze. "Forgive me for mentioning this, but you seemed rather taken with Mrs Cranford when we arrived."

Mr McRae's forehead creased. "Why shouldn't I be? I was being friendly."

"It's just that I didn't see her returning your attention. Was that usual?"

"Not when there were only the four of us, but we weren't

the only guests today. Of course she couldn't spend as much time with me ... us ... Betty and me, as she normally would."

"You didn't look particularly pleased at the time."

Mr McRae shrugged. "I didn't notice."

"Maybe you didn't, but your wife did. Could you tell us anything about your wife's friendship with Mrs Cranford?"

Mr McRae groaned. "If you're so observant, you must have seen it for yourself. Betty thought the world of her. She was always around here and wanted to do everything Ros did. She rarely waited for an invitation."

"And did Mrs Cranford mind that?"

"I couldn't say."

Eliza paused and bit down on her bottom lip. "Mr McRae, this is a rather personal question, but would you mind telling me about *your* relationship with your wife?"

Mr McRae stared at Eliza, his mouth open. "Aye, I would mind. What's it got to do with you?"

Eliza shifted in her chair. "The thing is, over luncheon I didn't see the two of you even acknowledge each other, except for one occasion when Betty became hysterical and Mrs Cranford asked you to talk to her. Had we not been introduced, I wouldn't have known you were acquainted with each other, let alone married."

"We were being sociable with the other guests; we spend enough time together at home."

"And yet despite that, you barely took your eyes off Mrs Cranford."

"I think you're imagining things."

Eliza raised an eyebrow. "Really? I was studying Betty earlier and realised that she and Mrs Cranford had very similar tastes in clothes and wore their hair in the same style.

Could it be that your wife was aware of your infatuation with Rosamund and was trying to make herself more like her to get your attention?"

Mr McRae threw back his head and released a humourless laugh. "You really have no idea. Betty is one of the most unlikeable women you'll ever meet. The thing is, she doesn't believe it and so for years she's copied Rosamund hoping it would fool people into liking her too."

Eliza stared at Mr McRae. *You can't say that about your wife!* "Well, I'm sure I don't know what to say. If she's so bad, why did you marry her? You must have liked her once."

Mr McRae hesitated as he glanced between Eliza and the sergeant. "Look, this really isn't any of your business, but let me be honest with you. My marriage to Betty is a sham, it has been from the start. Her father tricked me into it, promising me untold family wealth once we were married. Unfortunately, by the time I found out he was exaggerating, it was too late."

"You're saying you only married her for money?" Eliza's eyes were wide.

Mr McRae shrugged. "It seemed like a perfect compromise. I needed money to stay down here and her father was desperate to get her married off before she was too old. We managed well enough in the early days, but once we moved here everything changed. Ros took over our lives and Betty became infatuated with her. In fact, I'm rather concerned she's done something stupid."

The sergeant's brows drew together. "What do you mean?"

Mr McRae puffed out his cheeks. "It probably sounds ridiculous, but Betty's an incredibly jealous person. It had got to the stage where she wanted Rosamund all to herself, but naturally Ros wouldn't stop seeing her other friends. That was when Betty became 'difficult'. She hated it when Ros got the attention and she didn't ... and as you saw today, it wasn't easy to deal with. She could be as nice as pie in public, but once we got home, she would fly into a rage, throwing things and shouting about how everyone fussed Ros and not her."

"So, you think she was jealous of her?"

"I don't think she was, I know it. As much as she might tell you how much she liked her, she hated her too."

"Could she have hated Mrs Cranford enough to kill her?" the sergeant asked.

Mr McRae rubbed a hand across his face. "I don't know; I hope not, but I can't help worrying... She has been rather hysterical recently."

The sergeant's handwriting became hurried as he scribbled into his notebook before looking up. "And so you had no reason to want Mrs Cranford dead?"

Mr McRae leaned back in his chair, the rims of his eyes still red. "Believe me Sergeant, that's the last thing I wanted."

Eliza's mind was racing as the sergeant ushered Mr McRae from the room. *Grown men don't cry. Why was he so upset?* She still had the image of his tear-filled eyes in her mind when an idea struck her. *Could he and Rosamund have been more than neighbours?* She immediately shook her head. *No, they're both married and Rosamund didn't look the type to even consider anything like that.* She shuddered at the thought, but it was still troubling her when the sergeant returned with Archie. *Perhaps I'll keep it to myself for now.*

"How are you getting on?" Archie asked.

"Not very well, although I can't get Mr McRae out of my

mind. He seems far more upset than he should be. We need to speak to Mrs McRae again too."

The sergeant let out a sigh. "I suppose so, but I still have suspicions about Mrs Appleton..."

Archie burst out laughing. "You're not serious!"

"No, the sergeant's not, are you?" Eliza glared at Sergeant Dixon until he turned away. "He's just relying on the word of one witness and as soon as he can dismiss it, he will. Isn't that right?"

Sergeant Dixon checked his pocket watch. "It's turned seven o'clock. I need to get back to the station."

"What about Mrs McRae?" Eliza said. "We have to speak to her ... and Mr Cranford. We didn't establish whether he had a motive."

"I don't have time to do that tonight."

"Sergeant!" Eliza was on her feet pointing a finger at the wall between them and the drawing room. "There's a murderer in there. If we let them go home, the chances are whoever it is will disappear overnight and we'll never see them again."

The sergeant also stood up. "I'm sorry, but I need to leave and I can't lock everyone up until the morning."

"Well, you'd better send some men to patrol the area. This house and the McRaes' if I'm not mistaken, although you'd better have someone go to the Reeds' house as well, if you want to be on the safe side. I've a feeling they're not as innocent as they'd have us believe."

"I can't spare three men on a Sunday night."

"I've an idea," Archie said. "When I was in the drawing room, I was talking to Mr Cranford. He's rather shaken as you can imagine, and he asked if I could give him something to help him sleep. As soon as the ladies heard I had some sleeping draught at Mr Bell's, they wanted some too. If I give them all a dose, they'll be less likely to disappear and the sergeant can send some men over at dawn to make sure they don't do a morning flit."

Sergeant Dixon nodded. "It's certainly an idea, but do you think they'll all take it? I'm not sure Mr McRae and Mr Reed will be happy."

"I'm sure we can convince them of the benefits," Eliza's eyes narrowed. "Perhaps you should insist. Threaten to lock them in the police cells if they refuse!"

Sergeant Dixon scowled at her. "I would say that's a little drastic. Dr Thomson do you think you can persuade them to take enough to make them sleep?"

Archie nodded. "I would say so."

"I've another thought," Eliza said. "We should ask Mr Cranford to stay at Father's overnight. I'm sure he won't want to stay here on his own after everything that's happened, and that way we can keep an eye on him."

"So I'd only need two constables?"

"Precisely."

Sergeant Dixon turned to leave. "All right, let's tell everyone they can go home but I want them all back here at nine o'clock tomorrow morning. Anyone who fails to return will be treated as an absconding criminal."

CHAPTER TEN

E liza took her favourite seat by the fire in Mr Bell's drawing room and accepted the hot chocolate the maid handed to her.

"Thank you, dear." With the saucer resting on her knee she wrapped her hands around the cup and waited for the girl to serve Connie and Mr Bell. "Did you get a chance to put the bedwarmers in all the rooms? That wind's bitterly cold."

"I did, madam. The truth is, the weather was so bad, I didn't venture very far myself. I've been here for hours waiting for you."

"Bless you. It's such a shame to have your afternoon off spoiled but thank you anyway."

With a slight curtsey the maid turned and left the room.

"She's a nice girl," Eliza said. "Has she been here long?"

"A few months. In actual fact, Mrs Cranford found her for me. I'll tell her the details of Mrs Cranford's death tomorrow before she reads it in the newspaper. For now, I've said she died of natural causes and I want to keep it that way; we don't need anyone else not sleeping."

"No." Eliza took a sip of her chocolate. "Did you find out anything more about Mr Reed when you sat with him earlier?"

"I'm not sure how important it is, but Mrs Reed made an interesting comment."

"Go on." Eliza gave her father her full attention.

"Mr Reed had been complaining that thanks to Mrs Cranford he wasn't needed at church as much as he'd like. It seems he wants to be churchwarden, but Mrs Cranford had taken on responsibility for a lot of the tasks he wanted to do."

"Couldn't he have spoken to her? I'm sure she'd have understood."

"Perhaps she would, but Mrs Reed said he was upset after the events of today because he wouldn't have the chance to apologise to her."

"So you think they argued?" Connie asked.

Mr Bell nodded. "I certainly got that impression."

Eliza's forehead puckered. "Surely he wouldn't kill her because he wanted to be a churchwarden? It's not a very Christian thing to do."

"He does seem to have a temper though." Connie sat up straight in her seat, her drinking chocolate brought to a halt in mid-air. "And I imagine he usually gets his own way."

"It still seems rather drastic." Eliza glanced at the chair usually occupied by her husband. "I do hope Archie's not having trouble with him."

"I'm sure he's fine, he'll be home soon enough."

"I hope he's not giving all the sleeping draught away." Connie fixed her eyes on Eliza.

"Of course he won't. How are you feeling anyway? All that brandy must have done you some good."

"I suppose so, but it doesn't stop me thinking about poor Mrs Cranford ... or Mr Cranford. Do you think he'll be all right?"

"It won't be easy for him, but he has his daughter arriving on Tuesday; that should help."

"It might help him, but what about her? He won't even have time to write and give her the news."

"No." Eliza shook her head but immediately broke into a smile as the drawing room opened and Archie joined them.

"You're back. I was beginning to wonder where you were. Did Mr Reed put up much resistance when you offered him the sedative?"

Archie laughed. "You could say that. He was adamant he should be alert in case his wife needed him, but I managed to persuade him that he'd be more use to her if he had a good night's sleep."

"What about Mr McRae? Did he object?"

"No, not at all. In fact, he'd helped himself to a double dose before I could stop him and then he asked me to leave the bottle."

"You didn't, did you?" Connie's eyes flicked to Archie's medicine bag.

A smirk crossed Archie's lips as he lifted out a large glass container. "And leave none for you, you mean? Don't be silly."

Connie let out a deep sigh. "That's a relief ..."

"Come and sit down, I've been worried about you." Eliza stood up and plumped up the cushions on the settee.

"I'm sure I can look after myself. It's not the first time I've done house visits."

"That's all well and good under normal circumstances,

but the chances are one of those you've just visited is a murderer. That puts a whole new complexion on things."

"What if the killer's here?" Mr Bell raised his eyebrows. "We still don't know about Mr Cranford."

Archie took the hot chocolate Eliza handed him. "I wouldn't worry about him. I gave him enough sedative to make him sleep until the morning ... probably longer."

Eliza grinned and pulled a key from the pocket of her skirt. "And I locked his bedroom door once I knew he was asleep."

Mr Bell put a hand to his mouth to suppress a laugh. "I hope the chamber pot's still in there then."

The following morning, with the wind continuing to howl around the house, Eliza contemplated getting out of bed. She put an arm out of the bedcovers and swiftly pulled it back in again. The fire hadn't taken nearly enough chill off the room. She shivered and was considering spending another five minutes where she was when the sound of a door rattling across the landing brought her to her senses. *Oh my goodness, Mr Cranford! He doesn't know he's been locked in.*

Jumping out of bed, she hurried to find a robe. *Where's Archie when I need him? Why does he get up so early of a morning?*

"One moment, Mr Cranford," she shouted. "We must have accidentally locked the door last night. I'll ask my husband to fetch the key."

"Don't you go blaming me," Archie said two minutes later as he climbed the stairs to the bedrooms.

"It was only a white lie. I didn't want to upset him. Just give me a minute to get back into the bedroom and then you can let him out. I'll be down for breakfast shortly."

Mr Cranford was sitting at the dining table with Mr Bell and Archie when Eliza arrived downstairs.

"Good morning, everyone. Is there no sign of Connie?"

"No, not yet," Archie said. "I was hoping you'd check on her for me. She insisted I give her a rather large dose of sleeping draught last night and so she may be groggy."

"Oh dear, the poor thing; I'll go now. At least she'll have got some sleep."

By the time Eliza reached the top of the stairs, Connie was leaving her bedroom.

"Oh good, you're awake. We were beginning to wonder."

Connie shook her head. "I could have easily closed my eyes and gone back to sleep, but I remembered Sergeant Dixon saying that anyone not at the Cranfords' house by nine o'clock would be treated as an absconding criminal. I can't give him any more reason to suspect me."

Eliza put her arm around Connie's shoulders. "Don't be silly, he's not going to accuse you. I'll get Inspector Adams up here from New Scotland Yard if he shows any sign of blaming you."

A smile broke out on Connie's face. "Oh, what a relief, but why didn't you tell me last night? Then I wouldn't have needed such a big dose of the sleeping draught."

"I'm sure the sleep will have done you the world of good. Now, come along, Sergeant Dixon will be waiting for us."

When they reached the dining room, Eliza took the seat next to Mr Cranford. "How are you feeling this morning, sir?"

He gazed at the centre of the table. "Numb. That's the only way I can describe it. She was so full of life ... and now she's gone."

"And you can't think of a reason why anyone would want to hurt her?"

"No, none."

"It's such a terrible thing." Eliza helped herself to some toast. "Is there someone who'll open up the store for you this morning?"

"No, I always do the opening and closing myself. I need to get the carriage set up and go."

Eliza glanced at Archie and shook her head. Picking up on her signal, Archie gave a small cough.

"I'm afraid that's not going to be possible, Mr Cranford. Sergeant Dixon wants to speak to everyone again, and he gave me strict instructions to take you back to the house this morning."

Mr Cranford's eyes widened as he stared at Archie. "He can't think I had anything to do with it. I told him yesterday I didn't."

"We know that," Eliza said. "The problem is, there were a few more questions he should have asked."

"Such as?"

"Well, I'm not sure it's my place to say without the sergeant being here. I'll tell you what, why don't we finish breakfast and go to your house before the others arrive? That way you can speak to Sergeant Dixon first and he might then let you leave."

Sergeant Dixon was already in the drawing room when they arrived and Eliza wondered when anyone had found the time to put the furniture back into its original positions.

"The undertakers have been, I see." Archie nodded towards the place Mrs Cranford's body had lain.

Sergeant Dixon nodded. "Yes, you've just missed them."

"Where've they taken her?" Mr Cranford turned a full circle in the middle of the room. "She should be laid out in the front parlour."

"She will be, sir, but there needs to be a post-mortem," Archie said. "They'll bring her back ahead of the funeral."

"A post-mortem? She doesn't need one of those ... we're well aware of what happened. Well aware..."

Eliza waited for Mr Cranford to take a seat by the fireplace before she approached Sergeant Dixon.

"Sergeant, do you remember the questions we had for Mr Cranford yesterday? Could you possibly speak to him about them now? He says he needs to go into London to open up the store and so it would help if we could get them over and done with while it's quiet here."

Sergeant Dixon nodded. "I don't see why not; let me get him." He hesitated. "Will you join us?"

Eliza's face broke into a broad smile. "I'd be delighted to."

She followed them from the room, pursing her lips to suppress a smile when the sergeant reached into his pocket to retrieve the paper containing her questions.

"Now, Mr Cranford," Sergeant Dixon said, "if you don't mind, I'd like to ask about your relationship with your wife."

"What about it?"

"Well, I understand you didn't actually see much of her ... with you being at the shop for so many hours a day."

"We saw enough of each other and we were on good terms when I was at home."

Eliza sat forward in her seat and waited for permission to

speak. "It must be very exciting starting up such a prestigious store in the centre of London. Has it been successful?"

"Well, yes, I suppose you could say that. Why?"

The sergeant shifted in his seat. "It's just a precaution, you understand, but we need to check the store accounts to be sure you don't have any financial worries."

It was Mr Cranford's turn to squirm. "What do my accounts have to do with the death of my wife?"

"We don't know that they do, but the police need to take a look at them." Eliza kept her voice as level as possible. "The thing is, it's not uncommon for a murder to take place shortly after an insurance policy has been placed on the life of the victim ... especially if the perpetrator has any debts. Can we ask if you'd insured Mrs Cranford's life recently?"

"No, of course I hadn't. I needed all the money I could get to set up the store. There wasn't any spare for insurance."

The sergeant nodded. "I'm pleased to hear it but we'll check with the bank anyway, and we still need to see the accounts."

Mr Cranford glared at Eliza. "I don't know why you think I had anything to do with my wife's death, but I can assure you she meant more to me than any money. I'd give all I have to bring her back."

"Mr Cranford, we're sorry," Eliza said. "The sergeant just needs to eliminate you from his enquiries. He's looking for possible motives, but if you've nothing to hide, then you have nothing to worry about."

Mr Cranford nodded but remained silent.

"I think that's probably all we need from you for now," Sergeant Dixon said. "Could you return to the drawing room and wait for us there?"

The rims of Mr Cranford's eyes were red as he looked up. "I need to go to the store. They can't open without me and I can't afford to miss any business this week."

Eliza watched the sergeant as he flicked back and forth through the pages of his notepad.

"Very well. I'll grant you two hours to open the doors, but I want you back here before midday."

"Are you sure that's wise?" Eliza asked.

The sergeant nodded. "A man's innocent until proven guilty and I see no reason to ruin Mr Cranford's business if he's done nothing wrong. If it makes you feel better, I'll ask Dr Thomson to escort him ... just to be on the safe side."

Eliza nodded. "I'm sure that will be fine. Let me ask him for you."

CHAPTER ELEVEN

By the time Archie and Mr Cranford had left for London, Mr and Mrs McRae and Mr and Mrs Reed had arrived and were sitting around the fire.

"Are you going to keep us here long?" Mr Reed shouted to the sergeant.

"As long as it takes, sir, although I'm hoping we'll be finished in time for luncheon. I need to speak to Mrs McRae first, if you don't mind, of course, Mr McRae."

Mr McRae shrugged. "Be my guest."

Mrs McRae's glare could have frozen water, and she stood up and pushed past Mrs Reed on her way to the door.

"Shall we get this over and done with? I can't waste all afternoon here."

Eliza raised an eyebrow to the sergeant as Betty went on ahead.

"I'll be rather glad of your presence for this one." The sergeant caught hold of Eliza's elbow. "Would you mind starting the questioning?" His voice was low as they followed Betty into the morning room and took their seats.

"How are you feeling today?" Eliza asked.

Betty shot Eliza a venomous look. "How do you think I feel, less than a day after my best friend was murdered? It's going to take a lot more than a dose of sleeping draught to help me get over that."

"Yes, of course. I'm sorry. I can't imagine..."

"No, you can't. Your friend's still sitting out there with everyone else when she's the one who should be locked up." Mrs McRae took a handkerchief from the sleeve of her dress and dabbed at her eyes.

"Why do you keep saying that?" Eliza said, but the sergeant held up a hand to silence her.

"Mrs McRae, please. Can we keep this civil? What can you tell us about your friendship with Mrs Cranford?"

Betty waved her hand in the air. "What is there to tell? We were about the same age and enjoyed doing the same things. It was as if I had a big sister and I adored her for it. She was such a wonderful woman. I can't believe she's not here any more." She dabbed her eyes once more.

"Is that why you wanted to be like her? So that you'd be as popular as she was?"

Betty's head jerked upwards. "No, of course not. Who told you that? I've plenty of friends of my own."

"I'm sorry, I didn't realise."

"No, there's a lot you don't understand." Betty rested her hands on her lap. "I'm going to miss her dreadfully. I just don't understand how anyone could do such a thing."

"No, it's hard to fathom..." Eliza hesitated. "Look, I can see you're upset, but may I ask you about Mr McRae? The two of you don't seem to be on very good terms at the moment."

"What's that got to do with any of this?"

"It's just something he said yesterday…"

Mrs McRae's eyes narrowed. "What's he been saying? Is he the one who told you I have no friends?"

"Well, it's rather delicate, but he suggested that since you moved here … to Richmond … and since you became friendly with Rosamund … things haven't been the same between you and him."

"And he's blaming me?"

"Well, he said you spent a lot of time here and I got the impression you were with Rosamund more than you were with him. Could he have been jealous?"

Mrs McRae's face hardened. "Have you any idea why I was here so often? It was to stop him from visiting, that's why. He was infatuated with Ros to the point where he frightened her. I couldn't leave her on her own with him."

Eliza stared at Betty. "And you knew?"

"Of course I did. I always knew what Ros was doing; not that Cameron realised that. To start with, he would call around to see her when Mr Cranford was at work."

"And did Mrs Cranford encourage him?" Sergeant Dixon asked.

"Of course she didn't." Mrs McRae's voice squeaked. "She was my friend and wouldn't have done anything to hurt me … but he would." Her voice was cold. "He wanted to take her away from me, to a place where I couldn't find them."

Eliza's jaw dropped. "He told you that?"

Betty gave a firm nod. "He told me the night before the party that he was leaving Richmond and taking Ros back to Scotland with him."

Eliza sat back in her chair. *Good grief, I was right!* "Well, that certainly explains why you've not been speaking to each other. Was Mr Cranford aware of this?"

Mrs McRae's voice was again raised. "Of course he wasn't, there was nothing for him to know. Ros wouldn't have gone unless he'd forced her. She'd have stayed with me."

Eliza glanced at Sergeant Dixon whose pencil hung over his notebook.

"All right, let me get this straight," she said. "Your husband was besotted with your best friend and had told you that the two of them were planning on leaving Richmond together." She held up her hand when Mrs McRae tried to interrupt. "Please, allow me to play devil's advocate. What if Mrs Cranford intended to go with your husband? Perhaps she lied when she said she was frightened of being alone with him so that you wouldn't suspect there was anything going on. But you found out. After all, you've already said you knew everything she was doing. Would that give you a motive to kill her ... to save your marriage? It would be quite easy to take the fruit knife from the table once Rosamund announced what we'd be playing."

"Don't be ridiculous. Did you see my dress yesterday? It was a fitted garment, with tight sleeves and no pockets. Where would I hide a knife?"

"But you wanted her dead?" Sergeant Dixon asked.

"Of course I didn't. You can play devil's advocate all you like but I know she had no feelings for my husband, and she wouldn't have gone to Scotland with him. If I wanted anyone dead, it would be him..." Mrs McRae's fists were clenched tightly on her lap.

"All right, let's look at things another way," Eliza said. "What if Rosamund had told Mr McRae that she wouldn't go with him? Would that be a reason for him to kill her? Perhaps he thought that if he couldn't have her, nobody could."

"That wouldn't surprise me," Mrs McRae snarled. "He was always so selfish, always thinking of himself, he never once spared a thought for me." Suddenly her eyes widened. "You know, I do believe you're right. I imagine he told Ros of his plans, but she just laughed at him. He wouldn't have liked that. She'd have told him she wouldn't leave here because she'd rather be with me. He'd have been furious." Mrs McRae jumped to her feet. "Sergeant, you must arrest him, the man's a brute. I can't go back home with him."

"Calm down, Mrs McRae," Eliza said. "You spent the night together last night, and he didn't harm you."

"Only because I locked him out of the bedroom."

Eliza paused to stare at Betty. "You suspected him last night?"

"Not as such, but as you noticed, we weren't on the best of terms yesterday. What you said makes so much sense, though, and if he believes I was the reason Ros turned against him, I might be next on his list." Mrs McRae stared at Eliza. "You have to help me."

"That's enough." Sergeant Dixon slipped his notebook into the breast pocket of his uniform. "We'll speak to him again. Why don't you go back into the drawing room?"

"I can't go in there."

Eliza stood up and put an arm around Betty's shoulder. "All right, how about going into the dining room? I'm sure Mr Cranford won't mind."

Sergeant Dixon was waiting for Eliza when she returned to the morning room.

"What did you think of that?" she asked him.

"She's hysterical, clearly." The sergeant rocked back and forth on the balls of his feet. "If you ask me, I'd say she wants Mr McRae sent to the gallows."

"So you don't believe her?"

Sergeant Dixon laughed. "Not a word of it. In fact, it wouldn't surprise me if she killed Mrs Cranford so she could point the finger at her husband."

"That seems rather drastic ... to kill your best friend, I mean."

"It doesn't sound to me like she was her friend." The sergeant pulled a face. "Mrs Cranford was about to run off with her husband and she knew about it. Imagine the scandal. No, I would say it would be easier to kill Mrs Cranford rather than face the humiliation of her husband leaving her. The only thing is, she couldn't let him get away with it. What better way to make him pay than by accusing him of murder."

Eliza sighed. "I can't argue with your logic, but it sounds to me as if Betty preferred Mrs Cranford's company to her husband's."

"But she couldn't have killed him; he'd be too big for her, which might explain why she murdered Mrs Cranford instead.

Eliza paused. "We can't assume she's the murderer without any evidence. What if she's telling the truth? We need to speak to Mr McRae again ... and Mr Cranford. Let's see if he knew anything of the relationship between Mrs Cranford and Mr McRae."

The sergeant sighed. "Very well, let me go and fetch Mr McRae."

Eliza stared at Mr McRae as he entered the room. Had he slept in the suit he'd been wearing the previous day? Where had the smart businessman gone? He gave her an equally puzzled expression.

"What have you done with Betty? Has she confessed?"

"Would you expect her to?" Eliza asked.

"I-I don't know." Mr McRae looked to the sergeant, but Eliza didn't wait for a response.

"She told us about your relationship with Mrs Cranford. That you used to call here when she was alone and that the two of you were about to go to Scotland. Why didn't you tell us?"

The colour drained from Mr McRae's face and he slumped into the nearest chair. "I-I didn't think it was relevant."

Eliza couldn't hide the contempt on her face. "Not relevant?"

"I think you can do better than that, sir," Sergeant Dixon said. "It looks to me as if you had something to hide."

"No, I didn't ... I don't."

"So, are you going to tell us about it?" Eliza raised an eyebrow.

Mr McRae sighed. "If you must know, I'd told Betty the previous evening that Ros and I were leaving as soon as Christmas was over. Ros had the family coming for Christmas and she didn't want to upset them all beforehand."

"But you didn't worry about telling Mrs McRae?"

Mr McRae shrugged. "She'd been spoiling for a fight all day and I finally snapped. I couldn't help myself."

"So that's why you suspect she was the one who harmed Rosamund? To stop you from leaving her?"

"Good God, no. Oh, please excuse my language, but no. If she murdered her, it would be to make my life a misery, not to keep me here. She knew that making me stay with her would have been as good as killing me."

"She believes Rosamund would have stayed here, rather than going with you."

"She only said that because she refuses to see the truth. I knew how Ros felt about me."

"But if she refused to believe you, why would she take Rosamund's life? What if she was right and Rosamund had told you she wasn't going with you? I saw you disappearing into the hall together before luncheon and she seemed to be in a hurry to tell you something. Was that when you found out she wouldn't be going with you?"

"No, not at all."

"I imagine that if she had just rejected you it would have been very tempting to pick up a knife and slip it into your pocket. It'd be easy enough to do. Had you decided that if you couldn't have her, nobody else could either?"

Mr McRae banged a fist down on the table. "That's not what happened."

"So, tell us what did happen then." The sergeant sat poised with his pencil over his notebook.

Mr McRae pinched the bridge of his nose. "It wasn't like that. Ros was the most special woman I've ever known and yes, much nicer than my wife. We loved each other. The problem was, Betty never left her alone. She couldn't do anything without Betty watching her, but she was so nice, she put up with it for years. Finally, Ros admitted one night that she was tired of the constant attention and needed to get away. That was when I suggested we go together."

"And she agreed?" Eliza asked.

"Aye, she did. She wasn't sure at first, said she didn't want to hurt Mr Cranford, but he was so busy with the store that she never saw him. Eventually she agreed. I was obviously delighted and couldn't keep it to myself. That was why Betty was in such a foul mood yesterday. You must have noticed."

"I saw you escort her from the drawing room. Rosamund said she was ill."

"Yes, that's one way of putting it. I told you yesterday, Betty was terribly jealous around Ros and so when she was paying you so much attention, she realised Betty was becoming agitated and asked me to talk to her."

"Presumably she wasn't aware that you'd told Betty you were leaving. I'm sure you were the last person who should have been pacifying her."

Mr McRae shrugged. "There was no one else."

"What about Mr Cranford?" Sergeant Dixon asked. "Was he aware of any of this?"

Mr McRae shook his head. "Not about me and Ros."

"You're sure?" Eliza wished she was as confident as Mr McRae about Mr Cranford's ignorance.

"He knew about the problems with Betty, and Ros had promised to tell him we were leaving once the children had gone."

"And so you're not aware of any arguments between Mr and Mrs Cranford?" *If he knows, it puts a whole new complexion on things.*

"I can't say I am. As I said, Mr Cranford wasn't home often enough for them to argue and it troubled Ros. She wanted a man around the house."

"And so you've no reason to suspect he killed her?" Sergeant Dixon asked.

"No, but to be honest, even if he was angry with her, he

wouldn't hurt her. He loved her as much as I did." Mr McRae wiped his eyes with his handkerchief. "There's only one person who could have killed her, and she needs locking up."

The sergeant nodded. "I must admit, it would be heartless for a man to kill his wife days before the family were due home for Christmas."

Mr McRae put his head in his hands. "It would … almost as heartless as killing her in front of me. God, I'm going to miss her so much."

CHAPTER TWELVE

B y the time Eliza returned to the drawing room Connie and Mr Bell were sitting by the fire with Mr and Mrs Reed.

"Here you are, dear." Mrs Reed reached out her hand to Mr McRae as he ambled towards them. "Come and sit down. I've just asked the maid to bring through a pot of tea and some mince pies. I thought everyone could do with cheering up." She stared past Mr McRae to the door. "What have you done with Betty?"

Sergeant Dixon answered for him. "She needed some time on her own, so she's in the dining room."

"Do you know if Mr Cranford and Dr Thomson are back yet?" Eliza tried to keep her voice flat, but a knot tightened in her stomach.

"Not yet, but Dr Thomson said they'd be back in time for luncheon," Connie said.

"Well, it's to be hoped they hurry up, we need to go, don't we, dear?" Mrs Reed squeezed her husband's hand.

"What do you mean? You can't go yet." Eliza stared at the sergeant.

"There's a service in church this afternoon and we're on hymn book duty." Mr Reed's voice resonated around the room.

"Exactly," Mrs Reed added. "We can't let them down, especially now Rosamund won't be there."

"I would suggest we need an outcome to the case before anyone goes wandering off," Eliza said.

"If Cranford's gone, the rest of us should be allowed to leave too," Mr Reed snapped. "He could easily be the killer."

"That's why we asked Dr Thomson to escort him," Sergeant Dixon said. "To make sure he returns."

"And how do we know it wasn't the doctor? He's the only one here who would have known how to stab someone without making them bleed."

A shudder ran down Eliza's spine. "Don't be ridiculous. Doctors swear an oath to help people, not to kill them."

"That's enough, sir." Sergeant Dixon stood over Mr Reed. "We're doing our best to get to the bottom of this as quickly as we can."

"Well, you need to interview *her* again." Mr Reed pointed a finger at Connie. "As far as I'm concerned, she's still the prime suspect and yet she's not even being considered."

"And she hasn't shown us the ace of spades to prove she was the murderer in the game," Mr McRae added. "She could have been lying all along about tapping Mrs Reed on the shoulder."

"I was considered." Connie's voice pierced the room. "In fact, I was the first person questioned, but I've not been spoken to since because it's nothing to do with me ... and I *did* have that card, but even if I didn't, what does it matter? Nobody else has come forward with it."

Eliza held up a hand. "Connie, please, that's enough. Mr Reed's right. While we wait for Mr Cranford's return, we need to check your alibi and motive alongside some new information we've uncovered. Will you come with us?"

A short yelp left Connie's lips as Eliza headed for the door. She stopped and looked back over her shoulder. "Now, Connie."

The surprise on the sergeant's face turned to curiosity as Eliza indicated for him to join them.

"I've not done anything..." Connie squealed, as Eliza closed the door to the morning room behind them.

Eliza grinned. "I'm sorry about that, my dear, I just wanted the others to think we were about to interrogate you. I thought it would be easier for the three of us to talk in here, rather than in the drawing room with everyone else listening."

Connie put a hand to her chest. "You might have warned me. You frightened the living daylights out of me."

"I know, but I do have a few questions for you. I hope you don't mind, Sergeant, but Mrs Appleton has a knack of seeing things from a different perspective and I'm hoping she can help us. I must admit that at the moment I'm rather flummoxed by the conflicting stories we've been told."

Sergeant Dixon sighed. "I can't say I mind because I'm as confused as you, although I wish you'd waited until they'd brought the mince pies through. I didn't eat much for breakfast this morning."

"I'm sure we can rectify that." Eliza pulled a cord in the corner of the room that she presumed would ring a bell in the kitchen. "What would you like?"

By the time she'd finished telling Connie everything they'd learned, a tray of mince pies and a pot of tea had arrived.

"That's lovely, thank you." Eliza smiled at the maid. "Just leave it on the table and I'll deal with it."

"So Mr McRae's blaming Betty and she's blaming him?" Connie said once they were alone again.

Eliza stirred the teapot before adding milk to the cups. "That just about sums it up."

"So, who do you believe?"

"I don't know. It could be either of them…"

"But?"

Eliza smiled as she picked up the teapot. "But I'm worried we're overlooking Mr Cranford."

"Do you think he knew Rosamund was planning on leaving him?"

"It's a possibility, that's why I'm so keen to speak to him again." *If he comes back.* "I just hope he doesn't try to disappear."

"But even if he knew, would he kill Mrs Cranford because of it?" Sergeant Dixon set down his mince pie and wiped the crumbs from his mouth. "Wouldn't it make more sense if he'd confronted Mr McRae?"

Eliza nodded. "It would, although if Rosamund was determined to leave, the scandal could have ruined his business. How much better to be a grieving widower rather than a wronged husband."

Connie shuddered. "And he did look terribly upset. Remorse, do you think?"

Eliza shrugged. "It could be. Sergeant, how quickly can your men check up on Mr Cranford's business finances and the life insurance? I've an uneasy feeling about this and if he is our killer, I'm afraid he won't come back. We really need to find him as soon as possible."

"I've got a man stationed outside the house; I'll get him onto it straight away."

Sergeant Dixon picked up the remainder of his mince pie and left the room, pulling the door closed behind him.

"So, is that it?" Connie leaned back in her chair. "You think Mr Cranford killed his wife to prevent a scandal and possibly claim the life insurance money?"

Eliza sighed. "I can't say for certain, but I find it hard to believe that Betty or Mr McRae would have hurt Rosamund, given they were both so infatuated with her."

"What about Mr Reed?"

"What indeed?" Eliza took a sip of her tea. "He may be an opinionated fool, but I can't find a good reason why he would have killed her. Father didn't find out anything incriminating other than he'd had an argument with Rosamund about church duties. It's not much of a motive. No, the best I can come up with is Mr Cranford. I just hope he comes back to the house so we can speak to him."

Connie drained the tea from her cup. "Well, we're back to square one if he really does know nothing." She gave an involuntary giggle. "You know, if Rosamund and Mr McRae had run away together, I'd say Mr Cranford could have asked Betty to take Rosamund's place. I'm sure she could have taken over Rosamund's life if it stopped her from becoming destitute. As long as they stayed away from church, I'm sure nobody would have noticed."

Eliza clanked her cup back onto its saucer and stared at her friend. "Oh my goodness, Connie. That's it! You've just hit the nail on the head. We need to find Sergeant Dixon immediately. I think I know who the killer is."

Fifteen minutes later, Eliza was about to close the front door after Sergeant Dixon when Archie and Mr Cranford appeared on the garden path.

"You're back!" Eliza hurried towards them and took hold of Archie's hand.

"Of course we're back, I said we would be."

"I had my doubts, that's all." Eliza gave Mr Cranford a sideways glance, but he appeared not to notice. "I think I've worked out who the killer is. Sergeant Dixon's just gone to check something for me."

Archie's eyebrows rose. "Who do you think it is?"

"Shh. I'm not telling you here. Come inside and all will be revealed."

CHAPTER THIRTEEN

T he maid was clearing away a buffet of cold meats and cheese when Sergeant Dixon finally returned.

"I've missed luncheon?" His face fell as he stared at nothing more than a pot of tea and some petits fours that had been left on the sideboard.

Eliza was about to reply when Mr Reed strode down the room towards them.

"Where on earth have you been, Sergeant? Mrs Thomson seems to think she's in charge around here but Mrs Reed and I need to go to church. The hymn books won't hand themselves out."

"I'm sure there'll be someone who can step in for you, sir. For now, we need you here. If you'd take your seat, I'd like to start."

Mr Reed harrumphed and shuffled away as Sergeant Dixon scanned the room. "Good, we have everyone else. Let's get this sorted out."

"One moment, I'm sure you could do with this." Eliza

handed him a cup of tea. "Did you find what you were looking for?"

"Ah yes." He handed her a slip of paper. "I think it confirms your suspicions."

Eliza quickly scanned the document. "What a relief." A smile crossed her face. "Shall we go and tell everyone?"

"Don't we need to speak to Mr Cranford again?"

Eliza paused before shaking her head. "No, I think we'll find out what he knew as we go through the evidence."

"Very well." Sergeant Dixon marched to the fire and cleared his throat. "Ladies and gentlemen, thank you for your patience. If you'll take your seats, I'd like to put an end to this mystery."

"You know who took Rosamund from us?" Mrs Reed asked.

"We do indeed and if you'll indulge us for a few moments, Mrs Thomson will explain how we came to our conclusions."

Betty glared at her husband as she took a seat next to Mr and Mrs Reed on the left- hand side of the fireplace. Her husband appeared to ignore her as he sat opposite with Mr Cranford.

"Don't mind us," Archie said, as he and Mr Bell arranged several chairs opposite the hearth. "We'll only be a second."

Eliza nodded but waited until he'd helped Connie to a chair. "Right, thank you. I'll try to make this short, but as you know, this investigation hasn't been easy. It was only yesterday afternoon that Rosamund was stabbed to death in her own drawing room, but it was particularly puzzling because there didn't appear to be any reason for it. She was such a popular person, why would one of her close friends want her dead?" Eliza paused and glanced around at the eight pairs of eyes that stared back at her.

"Many people immediately thought that Mrs Appleton was the murderer. I must admit she had the opportunity to wield the knife, but then so did everyone else in the room."

"But not everyone else was found lying on top of poor Rosamund," Betty said.

"It wasn't me..." Connie squealed, but Eliza held up her hand.

"Of course it wasn't you. You'd met Rosamund at the same time as me, no more than two hours previously. You had no possible motive. That's why I knew we could discount you from the enquiries, even though others in the room insisted you were guilty ... perhaps to keep the attention away from themselves." Eliza stared to her right. "Isn't that right, Mr Reed?"

"S-she was on top of the body ... it must have been her."

Eliza cocked her head to one side. "Why would you continue to insist someone was guilty when it's clear they weren't? Who were you trying to protect? Yourself? Or perhaps your wife."

"Don't be ridiculous." Mr Reed was on his feet. "Rosamund was like a daughter to us, why would we hurt her?"

Eliza's eyes narrowed as she studied him. "Why indeed? Was it anything to do with the argument you'd had with her?"

"Argument! There was no such thing." Mr Reed turned first to his wife before glaring at the faces of those around him. "Who's been talking?"

"Perhaps it's time you did," Sergeant Dixon said. "What was the argument about?"

"There was no argument." Mr Reed stepped towards Eliza, but Sergeant Dixon grabbed him by the arm and indicated for him to sit back down.

"Another move like that, sir, and I'll have you locked up. Now, answer the question."

Mr Reed straightened his jacket. "All right, but it wasn't an argument. I just didn't like her doing so much work around the church. Ladies shouldn't be so busy and so I asked her to leave it for me to do. Unfortunately, she wouldn't listen and I needed to raise my voice to her."

"And what did she say to that?" Eliza asked.

"He made her cry." Betty fixed her eyes on Mr Reed as he stared at the floor. "He accused her of doing a poor job and told her to stay away from the hymn books."

"You made her cry over some hymn books?" Eliza couldn't keep the incredulity from her voice.

"You brute." Mr Cranford jumped to his feet but Sergeant Dixon stepped in front of him.

"That's enough, sir."

"Do you think he killed her because of it?" Betty's eyes were wide.

"Of course I didn't kill her." Mr Reed ran a finger around his collar. "It just wasn't one of the things she was good at. She never put the books the right way up. Some were upside down or back to front. It just wouldn't do."

"It's still a motive though." Betty's eyes narrowed as she glared at him.

"An unlikely one, I would say, but Mr Reed isn't the only one who may have wanted Rosamund dead." Eliza turned to Mr Cranford. "You had to be high on the suspect list."

"Me?"

"Why not? As I mentioned earlier, I'm aware of many a husband who's taken the life of his wife in order to claim the life insurance money. Why should you be any different?"

"Because I'd rather have Rosamund here than any amount of money."

Eliza nodded. "I'm pleased to hear it. I must confess, I doubted you earlier, but you'll be relieved to hear the bank have reported that no such policy was taken out. They've also confirmed the shop's finances are secure." Eliza patted the piece of paper she had placed in her skirt pocket. "That eliminates the most obvious motive you may have had for murdering Rosamund, but there is still another possibility. Did you take her life to stop her leaving you?"

"What?" Mr Cranford seemed genuinely perplexed.

"You didn't know?" Eliza raised an eyebrow. "While you were out, we learned that Mr McRae had asked Rosamund to leave Richmond and travel with him to Scotland."

"Is this true?" Amongst a chorus of disapproval, Mr Cranford turned to face a silent Mr McRae.

"What's up, aren't you going to answer Mr Cranford?" Betty glowered at her husband. "If you're too ashamed to tell him about your sordid little secret, perhaps I will."

"Shut up, woman. There's nothing to tell."

"Oh, so you're not so keen to talk about it now. It didn't stop you the other night."

Mr Cranford's eyes pleaded with Betty. "What aren't you telling me?"

Betty sighed. "I'm sorry to be the one to break it to you, but my husband asked your wife to elope to Scotland with him so they could one day be married. He said Ros had agreed to go, although I don't believe him for a minute."

"Rosamund was leaving me?" Incomprehension spread across Mr Cranford's face.

"Did you know anything of this?" Eliza asked.

"No, not at all. Not that I'd have let her go..."

"No, I imagine it would have caused quite a scandal if she'd left you for another man. It must be so much easier being a widower..."

Mr Cranford didn't move immediately but gradually he lifted his face to Eliza's. "Are you suggesting I killed Rosamund to stop her leaving me?"

"There are men who've murdered their wives for less. It's quite a motive."

"I've told you, I had no idea about any of this and you can't prove that I did."

Eliza took a step back, surprised at the conviction in Mr Cranford's voice.

"I may not have been the best husband in the world, but I would never hurt her."

"All right, then," Eliza said. "Let's assume Mr McRae had asked Rosamund to marry him, but you knew nothing of it. It still leaves Betty with a strong motive."

"No it doesn't." Betty's shrill voice cut through the air.

"It's more of a motive for killing someone than stacking a few hymn books wrongly, but you were happy enough to accuse Mr Reed. I would say you had more reason than most for wanting her dead."

"No, I did not! I told you, Ros was my best friend; she wouldn't have left me for *him*." Betty stabbed her finger in the direction of Mr McRae.

"Don't look at me," Mr McRae said. "I wouldn't have hurt her. I won't deny I wanted to take her to Scotland but Betty's fooling herself if she thinks she wouldn't have joined me. It was all arranged. Betty just couldn't accept it..." Mr McRae flinched as Mr Cranford lunged at him.

"That's enough." Sergeant Dixon prised the two men apart.

"All right, I think you've all said enough." Eliza glared at the group until there was silence. "We've established that Mr Cranford or Mr and Mrs McRae all had possible reasons for wanting Rosamund dead. On the face of it, Betty has the strongest motive. If Mr McRae filed for a divorce, it would have caused a terrible scandal, not to mention financial hardship. She also knew how much Rosamund's death would upset her husband."

Mr McRae nodded.

"The problem is she idolised Rosamund. She was everything Betty wanted to be and because she knew she would never be as popular, Betty decided that the next best thing was to imitate Rosamund and spend as much time with her as possible. Even from what I saw today, she clearly cared for Rosamund a lot more than she did for her husband. I would say that if Betty wanted anyone dead, it was probably Mr McRae."

Betty nodded as she glared at her husband. "Well, you've got something right."

"The thing is, Mr McRae felt the same way. When he told Betty he was leaving her, she flew into a rage, something we all saw the tail end of yesterday. I imagine she told him she would never grant him a divorce, as well."

Betty nodded again. "I did, not that I believed a word he said. I promised to tell Rosamund exactly what sort of man he is, in case she was in any doubt."

"The woman's deluded if she thinks she could stop me divorcing her..." Mr McRae spat his words out at Betty.

"Whether she is or not, if what you say is true, it was a risk you couldn't take." Eliza didn't take her eyes off Mr McRae.

"I wouldn't have killed Rosamund for that."

"No, I don't believe you would." Eliza paused as she held Mr McRae's gaze. "But you *would* have murdered Betty."

"But I didn't..." Mr McRae pointed at his wife.

"No, you didn't, but earlier today I remembered that you'd been staring at Betty and Rosamund shortly before the lights went out. You knew exactly where they were standing, but the problem was, once it was dark it became impossible to tell them apart. They were about the same height, similar weight. Betty styled her hair in the same way as Rosamund, and as if you needed confusing any further, they were wearing the same perfume. You were comfortable enough approaching either of them, but because you thought you were standing next to Betty, you put your hand across her mouth to stop her screaming. That was your mistake. If you'd heard her talking, you'd have known you had the wrong woman."

Mr McRae's eyes were wide. "You can't prove that."

"Oh, but I can. You see, you used such force on Rosamund's face that although there wasn't much of a struggle, there were faint markings where your fingers had been. I checked with Dr Thomson, and under the circumstances, we don't believe they could have been made by a woman. Given that we can discount Mr Reed and Mr Cranford, that only leaves you. I would suggest that the person you wanted dead was in fact your wife, but you accidentally killed Rosamund instead. That's why you knew exactly where to look when the lights came back on, and why you were so distraught when you saw who was on the floor. Sergeant, this is your culprit."

Eliza stepped back as Sergeant Dixon took hold of Mr McRae's arm and snapped one of the handcuffs on his wrist.

"Get off me. How can you say I wanted Betty dead? She's the mother of my children." Mr McRae pushed himself away from Sergeant Dixon and made for the door.

"Stop him." Archie jumped from his chair and raced to the door with Sergeant Dixon in pursuit. Seconds later, the sergeant grabbed Mr McRae, forcing him to the floor where he struggled to prevent his second hand being bound by the handcuffs.

"Leave me alone; haven't I suffered enough?"

Eliza watched from a distance until she spotted something on the floor. "What's that?" She hurried across the room and bent down to pick up a card that had fallen from Mr McRae's pocket. "Well, well, if it isn't the ace of spades. You've had this all along. Were you hoping it would divert attention to Mrs Appleton?"

Connie put a hand to her mouth. "How could you? What a horrible thing to do."

"I don't think he was singling you out, my dear." Mr Bell walked towards the group. "I've just remembered he was standing next to Mrs Reed when she fainted. I imagine it was him who wiped the blood on her skirt."

Mr Cranford pushed his way through the group. "Is that true? Come here, you blackguard." He grabbed Mr McRae by the jacket, pulling him to his feet. Without a second's hesitation, he swung back his right arm and aimed his fist squarely at Mr McRae's jaw. Mr McRae fell backwards and skidded across the room before crashing into the base of the Christmas tree. Time moved in slow motion as baubles and candles swayed with the impact but seconds later the tree crashed to the ground, burying Mr McRae, leaving only his feet poking out from under the star.

CHAPTER FOURTEEN

The following day Eliza and Connie arrived downstairs for breakfast just as the maid brought in a fresh pot of tea. Mr Bell and Archie were waiting for them.

"Did you both sleep well?" Mr Bell asked.

"Oh, I did." Connie helped herself to a slice of toast. "Dr Thomson must have given me so much sleeping draught the other night, I think it's still in my system."

Archie laughed. "I doubt that very much. You wouldn't have been able to get out of bed yesterday morning if I'd given you that much."

"I expect it's more the relief that you're no longer a suspect. You must have been worried." Eliza leaned over the table to inspect the colour of the tea in the pot.

"Yes, you're probably right. What a cheek of Mr McRae wanting to blame me though. What had I done to upset him?"

"You hadn't done anything, my dear." Mr Bell patted her hand. "You just happened to provide a useful diversion when you fell over the body."

"Hmm. Maybe I did, but what about him trying to incriminate poor Mrs Reed? There was no excuse for that."

Eliza picked up the teapot. "Desperate men do desperate things."

"Well, I shan't be playing that game again in a hurry. What a stupid pastime it is, anyway. I only agreed to it because you did." Connie looked at Eliza.

Eliza stopped what she was doing. "Don't blame me, I didn't want to play in the first place. There's a reason I was still by the fire when the lights were switched back on."

Connie chuckled. "You're not frightened of the dark, are you?"

"Of course I'm not." Eliza's cheeks reddened. "It's just that I'd rather not fall over something I can't see."

"Well, at least we've got it all out of the way before Christmas," Mr Bell said. "I was worried this whole affair was going to drag on for days. Well done for getting Mr McRae to admit he was the murderer too."

Eliza gave a subdued laugh. "It didn't take much, really. Betty was so angry with him, I suspect he thought he'd be better off confessing to the crime than going home."

Connie nodded. "She was furious, and quite right too."

"She seemed happy enough once he'd been taken to the police station. By the time I left, Mr Cranford had poured a couple of brandies and they were keeping each other company in the drawing room." There was a twinkle in Mr Bell's eyes. "In fact, I'd go so far as to say they were getting on rather well. I overheard him offering to take her to the store as his guest."

"My, how lovely," Connie said. "Did she accept?"

"She did; the last I heard, they were busy planning when to go."

Connie sighed. "I don't suppose we'll get our trip into town now. It's Christmas Eve tomorrow and then we're travelling back to Moreton the day after Boxing Day, which will be Saturday."

Eliza put her napkin on the table. "We could still go today. I don't think I'm up to shopping and going to the theatre but if we delay going home until Sunday we could go back into London on Saturday." She turned to Archie. "What do you think? Would Dr Wark mind if you're a day late getting back?"

"I don't suppose so. We're usually quiet at the weekend."

"Splendid! That's settled then. Why don't we go shopping today and go to the theatre on Saturday? In fact, why don't the four of us go?"

"Ooh, that sounds wonderful." Connie clapped her hands under her chin. "It's always nice to be escorted."

"What do you think?" Mr Bell asked Archie.

"What, about chaperoning two women around a shop?" Archie shuddered. "No, thank you! Besides, aren't we expecting Henry sometime today? Someone should be here to welcome him."

Eliza flicked her napkin at his arm. "Stop making excuses. Henry won't be here until later this afternoon and after the events of the last few days it will do us good to remember the Christmas spirit. If you get bored, you can always retire to a coffee shop and give us some peace and quiet."

Archie sighed in exasperation. "We'll be giving you peace and quiet? More likely it's the other way around. It's a good job there are some decent places around there."

A smirk crossed Eliza's lips. "So you'll come?"

Connie giggled as she looked at Archie. "You're just like Mr Bell used to be. Even when she was a young girl, Eliza could wrap him around her little finger."

Archie gave Mr Bell a crooked smile. "So, you're the one I've got to blame."

"Absolutely not. You've no one to blame but yourself."

"In that case, neither have you." Archie smirked as he pushed himself up from the table. "I suppose I'd better ask the stable boy to harness up the carriage while we're getting ready. At least it's stopped raining."

"This is going to be so much fun." Connie dabbed a napkin against her lips and stood up. "Let me go and freshen up. Don't go without me."

"As if we would. I still need to sort myself out, anyway." Eliza was about to stand up when there was a knock on the front door. "Oh no. I hope this isn't Sergeant Dixon with more questions. I thought we'd gone through everything yesterday afternoon..."

A moment later a young man with dark brown hair and a full smile popped his head around the door. "Still at the breakfast table at this time!"

"Henry!" Eliza jumped up to plant a kiss on her son's cheek before he could duck out of the way. "What are you doing here? I wasn't expecting you until tonight."

"And miss out on a murder investigation! Did you hear that someone around here's been stabbed? It was in the late edition of yesterday's paper."

Mr Bell laughed as he shook his grandson's hand. "What do you think? Are there any murders in London nowadays that your mother doesn't know about?"

"As if that's my fault." Eliza put a hand on her son's shoulder. "But you needn't worry. I'm pleased to report that the culprit's in prison and we're going into London for a day out."

"You mean you don't need any help?"

"Not unless you want to be a porter. Connie and I have a rendezvous at Cranford's department store and we may need some assistance."

"Oh." The smile dropped from Henry's face.

"Don't be like that, you should be pleased the killer's behind bars and we can enjoy Christmas. Now, if you want all the details, you'd better keep your coat on. We'll tell you about it on the way."

*

Thank you for reading! I hope you enjoyed it.
If you did, I'd be grateful if you could leave a review on
Amazon.

Reviews are important because they help books gain visibility
and can bring them to the attention of more readers who may
enjoy them.

To leave a review, just search for
'VL McBeath' in the Amazon store, click on the book and
scroll down to the review section where it says
'Write a Customer Review'.

My only plea. Please no spoilers!

*

The next book in the series is
A Scottish Fling

Eliza, Connie and Henry join Archie as he visits his family in
Scotland ... but murder isn't far away.

For further details, visit my Amazon Author page.

Thank You!

AUTHOR'S NOTE AND ACKNOWLEDGEMENTS

It didn't occur to me when I was planning this book quite how difficult it would be to write a Christmas story in the middle of summer! Not that British summers are anything to get excited about, but I did sit on the patio with my laptop on a number of occasions and it felt decidedly strange.

The other thing I hadn't thought through properly was having Rosamund as the murder victim. Those of you who've read previous books will know that I tend to kill off nasty characters, but I'd had a few comments from readers and so I thought, 'why don't I surprise people and kill off someone nice!'

While there may be some merit in doing that, to do it in a Christmas book was probably not one of my better decisions - at least not while I was writing it! Fortunately, from early feedback, I think it worked quite well, but it's something I'll think about when planning future books.

As always, I'd like to thank my family, friends and advanced review team for reading various drafts of the book and giving me feedback. Particular thanks must go to Erin Janes for helping with some of the details around the murder scene. If there are any inaccuracies in the text, they are because of my creative license to make the facts fit the story, rather than any inaccuracies on her part!

Finally, thank you for reading.
I hope to see you for the next book!

ALSO BY VL MCBEATH

Eliza Thomson Investigates:

A Deadly Tonic (A Novella)

Murder in Moreton

Death of an Honourable Gent

Dying for a Garden Party

Look out for the newsletter that will include details of launch dates and special offers for future books in the series.

To sign up visit: https://www.subscribepage.com/ETI_SignUp

The _Ambition & Destiny_ Series

Based on a true story of one family's trials, tribulations and triumphs as they seek their fortune in Victorian-era England.

Short Story Prequel: _Condemned by Fate_

(available as a FREE download when you get Part 1)

Part 1: _Hooks & Eyes_

Part 2: _Less Than Equals_

Part 3: _When Time Runs Out_

Part 4: _Only One Winner_

Part 5: _Different World_

For further details, search 'VL McBeath' in the Amazon store.

Printed by Amazon Italia Logistica S.r.l.
Torrazza Piemonte (TO), Italy